# Attack of the Koto Maru

## By

## Alan De Wolfe

Copyright © 2001 by Alan De Wolfe
All rights reserved.
No part of this book may be reproduced, stored in a retrieval system, or transmitted by any means, electronic, mechanical, photocopying, recording, or otherwise, without written permission from the author.

ISBN: 0-75962-831-9

This book is printed on acid free paper.

1stBooks - rev. 4/4/01

# CHAPTER ONE

Paul Stevens had piloted his one man skiff through this South Pacific Island chain for four years. Evening would soon be upon him on Catena, the island farthest north and Paul was a little further up the beach than he usually wandered.

The former New York investment broker reckoned this remote outpost was a private island. The carefully kept coastal road indicated somebody had cash to burn. The high wall protruding ominously from a hilly escarpment fortified that notion.

On a previous visit he'd observed a sports car zooming along that same road and wondered about the logistics of maintaining a car here, hundreds of miles from civilization. Such a road would be a special accomplishment, even for the rich. But a nice car deserves a nice road improbable or not and the owner probably didn't care. As far as he knew and from what he could see, the road circumscribed the island. There was money here all right, by the buckets. And probably lots of security equipment.

As Paul stepped along in the shifting surf his instincts told him he was being observed. At this moment he sensed the presence of electronic surveillance devices pointed at the beach and at a certain independent vulnerable American who never could leave well enough alone. Was he imagining it? Curiosity had made him smart in business, but curiosity sometimes had a down side and the thought of being watched by cameras tended to make him a careful guest. It made him hope that the owner of this lush, lonely island wouldn't mind if he stopped occasionally.

Among lofty palm umbrellas high on a cliff out of sight one of the security workers peered from a sweaty-hot bunker. The large man swung his stout Polynesian bulk away from the periscope lens and said, "There is that American-looking man again. What shall I do?" His superior smushed a banana between his teeth and spoke from a sprawled position. "We've seen him before, but I don't trust him. He looks like a rich American with nothing to do, but do not take your eyes off him."

"They are very spoiled, with all their money."

"Don't worry, my friend. That will make the Prince's surprise much better!"

"Of course. You are correct, ha, ha!"

With sundown about to blaze, Paul's curiosity finally took a wrong turn. His movement through the darkened hedgerow nearby would be obscured from the cameras if there were any, and if his pounding heart didn't give him away. It was time to make a shift off the beach and into the thick flora to look at the wall he'd seen only from afar. The constant motion of life on the high seas was beginning to lose its influence in his mind. His land sense was returning. The surf on the seaward side of his body splashed itself silver in its run toward his hastening feet. It seemed to whisper a warning.

He slipped carefully into the cover of brush and odd little trees and walked inland amid the heightening sounds of evening. Moving steadily upward he crossed the paved roadway then proceeded through the jungley tangle of undergrowth. He cut furtively in and out of the brush cover under a dark palm canopy until reaching the base of a steep hill. What he saw next caused a quiver of fright to descend his backbone.

Near the top of the hill, the wall of concrete he'd noticed from a distance came straight out of the grassy surface and ran for more than two hundred feet. It gave the impression of a World War II bunker with long slit windows placed here and there for observing the bay. And it was much more frightening up close. For Paul, it was nearly impossible to fathom the immensity of the structure, and equally impossible to ignore the prick of danger stimulating his taut nerves. The wall was overpowering and sinister when viewed from the very bottom. It seemed to be falling over on him.

He began to climb the grassy embankment through vegetation getting sparser with each step. The climb was not easy with its angled and difficult footing, but his bare foot pads seemed to grip the dewy surface well. After ten minutes of heavy breathing he lifted his glistening body slowly over the crest. The sight was hard to believe.

His eyes widened when the concrete slab on top of the bunker showed its open sprawl hundreds of square feet straight ahead of him. At the center of the "top" was a big hole open to nature and like a crab on a beach, Paul skittered to the interior edge of the gigantic abyss. As he neared the rim to look within its confines, the stars seemed to appear unexpectedly in an otherwise lightless sky. He looked up, and around, and wondered why he was exactly where he was.

The heaving swells of emotion ebbed and flowed in his gut while his stealthy crawl brought him nearer to the hole's edge. The blackened night sky above him and the opening seemed to issue warning.

In a moment, his astonished vision trickled over the hole's edge and into a light so strong that it struck his face with a warmth of its own. Inside the bunker and directly under him he saw a dozen or more white-suited men busily working among cubicles and dividers. Unlike mice in a box, each technician seemed to work with great purpose in a murmuring technobabble of scientific jargon and foreign accent. Paul couldn't place the accented English but his karma told him something was diabolical about the scene. Though unnoticed above them, his breath stopped in his throat and he got that peculiar sleep feeling in his crotch.

"What the hell..." he whispered.

From the roof it was easy to see other buildings and abutments around the perimeter of the large open-top bunker as if standing to guard it. The whole thing had the look of unfriendly fortification. Paul's stomach knotted tight and brought his own vulnerability forward in his mind.

"Jeez...I can't believe this!"

Off in the distance, way beyond the endless roof he could see a splendid house of concrete and marble glowing in hues of pink in the day's ending moment. It was at nearly at the same level as the concrete's flat top and seemed to command the entire island with its presence. A landing pad lay near the house with several helicopters reflecting the strengthening twilight like malevolent blue crystals. A man who had his own chopper squadron was wickedly unsettling to Paul. He figured the harbor to be directly below the house in a convenient fold of curved earth. The only action at the house was a set of headlights leading his eye down the road from the house to the harbor till they disappeared. He focused again on the hole in the bunker and let his eyes spill over the edge.

Gazing down on the partitions he observed the two main rooms where six or seven men attended a sort of machine. It was about six feet long and three feet wide with a curved top open to facilitate their labors. There were other machines nearby causing much conferring and dashing to other rooms for discussions. Paul experienced a quick chill remembering the cameras seen earlier on fixed poles above the bunker's roof line and got the cold clammy feeling that sooner or later he'd have to explain himself. The devices seemed to be pointed out to sea but he couldn't be sure they weren't spying on him right this minute. He couldn't see them easily from his prone position, and he hoped they couldn't see him.

As he lay flat observing the action below, a shocking snap occurred directly under his stomach. A rolling metal roof began playing out from beneath his chin causing his bones to rattle and vibrate somewhere inside him. He recoiled into a standing position. His anxiety escalated into near-panic. The green and white surface resembled a tennis court. He whispered to himself. "Camouflage?"

The rumble of metal against metal cloaked his scurry to the wall of the enclave and to the building's side structures. The thought of being discovered in a place he shouldn't be still flew around in his mind like a flight of bats.

"Oh God, what next?"

He flipped his body off the roof exactly where the wall jutted out from the grassy hill in the very same moment the roof clicked shut. With his back hard against the wall, relief and fright mixed unwillingly in his mind. He noticed a bay window arrangement near him on the bunker's side beckoning at least a quick look before he went any farther. The glass panes were dark red and showed guards sitting at their equipment inside. He wasn't sure what caused the surge of bravery, but intuition convinced him to sneak even closer.

A cautious slide brought him a few feet along the wall and slightly down the hill in absolute silence. Shifting one foot past the other to get as close as possible to the window before the landscape dropped off, he prayed the grass hadn't gotten too damp for his foot grip. The darkness had deepened and before he saw it, a camera presented its blinking side to his close stare. His unwilling eyes were suddenly one inch from the camera's side. An expletive oozed through his teeth.

"Damn!"

From slightly above his eyes, the camera panned the entire length of beach below where his hapless boat lay bobbing in easy surf. Easing under the camera, he shifted again along the wall to a corner of the darkish window arrangement designed to jut out from the rest of the wall. He knew it might give him a better perspective and he was right.

His brow shined in sweaty reflection on the glass, his chin released a droplet which dripped on his knee. Inside, a man walked quickly past the window, shocking him so much he stiffened like a corpse. The burly man joined a companion sitting relaxed by a pile of banana peels and bantered with him in a language other than English. Control panels blinked as if idling. The rosy glass made them all twinkle red and added a surreal color to the dark sweaty men inside.

The bizarre setting gained authenticity when one of the men moved aside to reveal a sight Paul found unbelievable. Beyond the control panels, well past the reclining men, shore cannons of enormous proportion loomed high on a girded platform poised to deliver their ordinance far out to sea. Paul again muttered unwillingly under his breath.

"What the hell...?"

All the things he had seen to this point paled in the overpowering presence of these gleaming gun barrels. He guessed them to be British, possibly off an old gunboat. "What kind of place is this?"

Gripped by alarm, Paul backed carefully under the camera, made his way to the hill's steep edge and slid down it quickly on his backside. Under twilight slipping away faster than he could descend, his thoughts whipped him into a frenzied run. With his own fear chasing him, he tore through the familiar hedgerow of trees and bushes with no regard to the whipping, scraping motion of weeds, lacerating and bloodying his bare legs. Alarm's great infusion of adrenaline had hit his body with unrelenting force. The focus of the night, the creatures of the night and the hard snapping debris under his feet continued to heighten the dread he felt being the only observer in a place of obvious evil. His mind kept telling him, "Can I get off this island fast enough?"

## CHAPTER TWO

Susan Black opened her eyes. Her first sensation was a pounding headache followed by pain in her two delicate wrists. Coarse rope bound her tightly, sticking through her skin with stiff hemp fibers. Through the windshield she could see a small plastic hatch in the "ceiling" of the odd tomb, issuing forth a single stream of bright light. It seemed odd that her feet were not bound. Had she been drugged?

The air was cool but her thin sweater and cotton blue jeans were sufficient to ward off the shivers. A blanket was swirled at her feet. Under her shapely bottom was Corinthian leather she had felt once before at an Italian car dealership. It took only a moment to notice, she was sitting reclined in the passenger's seat of a silent Ferrari. "Am I dreaming?"

A train of thoughts began a wild run through her mind in spite of the drowsy effects of sedation.

"Is Louie dead? He was the last one to see the information - some mad scientist's shopping list of cylinders, gizmos electronics and worst of all, plutonium. I never thought the rats would kidnap me!"

She spoke aloud, "Oh, man! Did the paper get to Rear Admiral Jessup?" Her head popped alive with questions and bewilderment. "Because if it didn't, I'm dead!"

Bits and pieces of her abduction faded in and out of her conscious. How could she have been so careless? With hindsight she uttered, "I wasn't careless. They stalked me!"

She unlatched the car door and bent her body toward the opening. Over a soft leather kick panel she exited the car unsteadily and moaned herself into an erect position. In a moment, the strange unnatural movement that caused the automobile and the odd enclosure to tilt weirdly and pitch to and fro, moved her and her bewildered body to a rusty wall. She braced herself and tried to think it through. "I'm on a ship!" she cried.

Susan worked her way over to a slit in the huge steel container and peered out past its jagged edge. She could see that the box she occupied was in the top row of a stack of steel containers aboard a slow-going freighter somewhere in the middle of an awful lot of water. Worst of all, probably no one at her office had any idea she was missing. The stark reality of her situation hit hard and gave her a terrible thought. She might never be seen again! Her mind slipped into a survival mode.

On a table just behind the car she noticed some food packages in a tied-down wicker basket. A note read:

Good evening, Ms. Black,

By now it is June 23, assuming you wake up on schedule. There is enough food in these packages to sustain you until we reach our destination. I suggest you contemplate your position. No harm will come to you as long as you are prepared to obey me.

She read further:

I am Ranar Moolong of the Pacific nation of Malua. You and the car are my possessions. It's useless to make noise, for everyone on the ship is in my employ. A surprise awaits you, which I hope you will find most pleasant.

Alarm bells sounded along the pathways of her nerves creeping through her body like the growing morass of some unwanted nausea. She fell back against the car dazed, still grasping the note, not knowing why her mind suddenly recalled those early years in Cincinnati, when a too-thin girl won the highest honors bestowed any student in the history of the city school system. Not only smart was she, but the year's homecoming title fell in her lap underwriting the awakening confidence her parents had always tried to nurture. After college, she'd secured a career at the nation's number one information center, the Pentagon and got to deliver "things" in a briefcase handcuffed to her wrist. It had seemed like fun to her. But not today. "Why did they make a pigeon out of me?" she wondered, remembering the paper she had consented to deliver to Louie. "Friggin' CIA," she muttered. "Who knows what the hell they're ever up to!"

She looked again at the lower deck through the slit in the wall. Below, a door opened and a tanned, black-haired man stepped out. He stood at the base of the stern-located superstructure and engaged his men in a hurried expression of officious dialog. The vertical part of the ship towered high over him and its wheelhouse was nearly eye-level to Susan's peek hole. He wore a turtleneck shirt and looked regal enough to be important to somebody. It was impossible to hear what was being said but the crew members seemed to address the man in a very respectful manner. The crewmen bowed after each conversation and backed away, somewhat prostrating themselves as if leaving the presence of royalty.

With princely stride, the dark-haired man left the main deck and gave a look upward at the container. It caused Susan to duck, though she quickly realized he could not actually see her. Through the narrow slit, she peeked again. The man below exited the deck through a hatch and faded from sight, giving orders as he went in a language not familiar to her.

Gazing again at the bright blue sea, the woman from Cincinnati wondered what lay beyond its laser-flat horizon. Again she contemplated her desperate situation drifting off into the blue sky with the circling gulls. She felt a certain identity with the birds. What if there were no ship under her? She and the birds would be far from any convenient solid object. "I've got no choice," she mumbled. "I've got to see it through."

About an hour later, and after a lot of introspection, Susan noticed a sharp edge on the inner wall of the container. She quickly rasped her tethers into frayed fragments which eventually fell from her wrists. Her hunger caused her to attack the packs of food and the jug of water. She ground some potato chips between her teeth and rolled gently with the ship, heaving and pitching, still in deep thought.

Thirst gave her reason to wipe the grease from her hands and quaff a healthy swig of water. After the cooling drink she focused on a hinge along the bottom of the wall in front of the Ferrari. It wasn't difficult to figure how the container might open and what she could do to even the odds a little. The car was tied down with heavy rope and she reckoned that the box was air-conditioned not for her, but for the fancy automobile. The car's fuel tank was full and the ignition keys sent a startling flash of light into her retinas. "Ah, ha! The keys are in it." She sat down once again on the soft leather to daydream about a plan to get herself out of the present mess. The spark of an idea played across her searching mind. "It could work."

Half a world away at the Pentagon, Rear Admiral Jessup, glanced out the window and spoke with one of his staff underlings. Jessup, never much of a commander, loved to exhibit his bully power.

"So what if the guy bought plutonium? Anybody can get it now."

Lieutenant Mark Ingram decided to confront him. "But sir, you know yourself plutonium is almost always used in the fabrication of atomic weapons, and this guy is royalty, one of the richest men in the world. Who knows what he might be capable of?"

"The making of weapons is not always the case," his commander roared. "Get me some proof before you expect me to send in the troops. Hell, he's got a reactor on that island, Malua or whatever it is, to provide electricity for his kingdom, maybe he needs it for that. What can I do?"

"Sir, we have reason to believe that this Ranar has a private island somewhere far removed from his home country. I need people to help establish an investigation!"

"I'm sorry, Lieutenant, you'll have to do better than that! Now, I have a one o'clock meeting with Admiral Robertson's staff so if you're finished..."

*Attack of the Koto Maru*

"Yessir, finished...for now."

A disappointed Lieutenant Ingram walked from the admiral's meeting room with a concerned scowl. The paper in his hand was a detailed printout of purchases made by Ranar Moolong giving strong hint that they would be applied to making atomic weaponry. To Mark, even the possibility of anyone using them for weapons couldn't be tolerated. The possible weapon application seemed very obvious to him, despite the fact that all materials could be used for peaceful purposes. Mark maintained a certain dread about it.

C.I.A. operative, Louis Nugent, had expressed his concern that one of the secretaries might have been kidnapped because of her role as courier. "The poor girl would have been an innocent pawn," Mark reckoned. "I hope it's not true."

It also increased his anger to know that Louis had told him that the last page of the document had included a map of Moolong's private island and most important, the location. Unfortunately the map was lost from the report and would have given the paper much stronger credibility. If an American's life were in danger, it would surely add to the importance of the map. He sensed that finding the island must soon become his number one imperative even if no one felt like cooperating. He was infuriated by the offhand attitude of "The admiral". "And what's he trying to feed me anyway? Those guys he's meeting with aren't members of Robertson's staff. I oughta know!"

Back down the corridor a few feet Rear Admiral Jessup closed his conference room door. Immediately, one man in the room flustered and sweating said, "What are you going to do about him, he's seen all four of our faces!"

"Believe me gentlemen your faces will fade from his memory when he sees all I gave him to do this week."

Another said, "I don't like it, anyway! Suppose he really thinks about it in depth. He's bound to reach some conclusions."

"Gentlemen, gentlemen, don't worry. He still has to go through me for anything he does. He's at a standstill, believe me."

The admiral's words didn't set well with the three men in the room smoking ten-inch cigars in a nervous snit. Each one a career naval officer, they realized everything depended on the covertness of their dealings with the man who'd brought them this far along - Admiral Jessup. If but one thing were found out, the whole shebang would likely be revealed and their careers would be over. It occurred to Admiral Jessup that there were three different smells of perspiration in the room. They tended to sour the mix of after shaves, he thought as he chortled past the smoke of his own cigar.

To the admiral, Mark may have seemed powerless. But the clever lieutenant hadn't spent thirteen years in the Pentagon without learning some special skills. The thing that bothered Mark most was that someone's life might be in danger. "Not that pretty secretary Susan...mm what's her name?" he mumbled in a daydream. "That would indeed be a tragedy. At least she and Louie got me the information, and I'm exactly the one who should have it."

Mark had been a New York City kid from the Bedford-Stuyvesant section who boxed at a local gym to guarantee his safety on the streets. The "bed-sty" pugilistics made him strong and resolute as a kid and as an adult. He dealt strongly but fairly with others. A startling experience in faith humbled him one day, and seeing it personally was the start of a restructured life. It proved far preferable to the direction he seemed to be headed. In those difficult high school years, a time when he knew more of trouble than school work, his morality teetered on the brink of steep descent into the pits of darkness. What's more, he'd begun to drink.

One evening, nursing a drunk's headache and a cut eye he'd walked into a soup kitchen not far removed from his neighborhood where a "healer" was preaching.

"Mabel, come here!" the healer stated with gusto. "The Spirit is here tonight and your sight will be returned to you."

*Attack of the Koto Maru*

Mark's attention snapped round to the front of the room to a woman he'd known quite well. Mabel, a local blind lady and friend of his family's for years shouted, "I'm coming, Lord!"

Mark had wanted to run up and punch the so-called healing trickster for leading such a fine lady into false hope. He'd stayed back until Mabel, stumbling as usual needed his help. For a reason unknown to him he'd quickly cradled her arm.

"Here, I'll help you, Mabel." Privately he'd imagined the unfortunate lady would continue her life unsighted. The healer's cockiness again had angered him.

On that night in the homeless kitchen he remembered pulling her arm gently and leading her to the front of the healer. A few soft words were said while he held Mabel upright in the influence of the healer. He hadn't wanted to be there and immediately looked away, but he managed to glance back in time to see a strange expression cross Mabel's face. The healer placed his hands on Mabel's eyes and the woman nearly fainted.

After regaining herself, she looked straight ahead and began to weep. Her black perceptions lightened into shades of gray as the veil of blindness apparently lifted from her face. Colors were happening in her conscious focus and were becoming clearer by the minute! She finally shouted something Mark never got out of his mind. "I can see!"

Among the people taking refuge in the soup kitchen that night, the monastic silence had come apart when everyone who'd seen it started to applaud and sing praises for her miracle. Mabel could smell the booze on Mark's breath as she turned to his unsteady body and said quietly, "So that's what you look like, Mark Ingram."

Mabel's abrupt sightfulness made Mark feel he'd suddenly been shaken by God out of a life of indulgence. He couldn't explain what happened, but he knew he'd played carelessly with what his new found Creator gave him instead of handling it correctly. Mabel's new, twinkling deep eyes had shocked him back from the murk of drunken tomfoolery to a place of reverence at her feet. Little more could be said when she helped him to his feet that evening. But it turned his life around.

# CHAPTER THREE

"Father, it's time to let the secret be known."
"No, No, my son! Must remain secret!"
"But father..."
"No but! Leave alone!"
Naoki (Now-kee) Matsumoto was weary of the big concealment shared by nearly all thirteen hundred souls on the island of Timano. His home was the southern-most fragment of land in the chain, being about eight hundred miles northeast of the Solomon Islands and due south of Midway Island. "Why not tell the world of this. I'm thirty-two and I'm tired of this cultivated secret," he thought, sinking into sarcasm. "Hasn't it been long enough, some forty-five years, actually predating my birth in this tropical paradise, that this has been going on?"

Naoki had tried before to persuade his father and indeed all the old men, that the world would forgive their hoary old secret, but the elders would have none of it. "I can't just let it go forever, not when it could put our island on the map really good. I'm sick of being so backward!"

The younger adults on the island were adamant about wanting to reveal their mystery to the world, that they might encourage tourism and "join the twentieth century." But such thinking was directly contrary to what the elders wanted. Oblivion was what the old folks desired and oblivion was what they had. The "kids", most of them in their mid-thirties and most with their own families, were at constant odds with the respected old people. Even the usually reasonable women wouldn't budge. "Hmmph, our sons and daughters could go to school in the states if someone would take this island seriously. Of course, money and talent helps too."

Naoki was aware of the outside world because of the teachers who had come to the island and departed and from the glut of books and magazines sugar cane buyers often brought them. He had never been away from Timano except to some

*Alan De Wolfe*

neighboring islands within his chain of seamounts, but his friend Ningo Kyoshi had, and the tales he returned with were no balm to his growing unrest. "It's ridiculous that we should remain so isolated."

The island had experienced an influx of the English language from U.S. teachers who had been invited in by request of the elders after the war. The islanders, at least the young ones, consumed it voraciously along with all the idiosyncratic trappings that went with it. Rock and roll was well known, Broadway shows were talked about and American youth were admired for their swagger and savvy. When the contracts were finished and the teachers left, the population never completely reverted to its former ways instead finding itself left with a gaggle of young people who were thoroughly westernized and crying for more. The young now spoke mostly English and would continue U.S. tutoring methods amongst themselves. Lately, they could see a lot of U.S. television via satellite linkup which unfortunately for the elders, made their young citizens pine for even more western culture, specifically U.S.

After being on Timano fifteen years it was more and more difficult to get U.S. teachers to continue in such pervasive isolation. Eventually, as commitments ran out, the foreign educators could stand no more and fled the boredom. No new teachers came because the money had stopped. The paradise of Timano Island was essentially broke.

The teachers had left an indelible mark on Naoki and his friends through their early years as teens and paved the way for a complete understanding of American culture. Among the young people of Timano, idioms and slang were thrown around with abandon at their nightly campfire gab sessions.

Naoki's island might be considered a nirvana to the world-worn people of today except that it was never developed at all. The homes of the people were sturdy abodes appearing here and there among the trees built of native timbers and giant palm fronds, but the people who build hotels and resorts had passed

*Attack of the Koto Maru*

them by. Small outbuildings completed the look of tropical ambiance much like a movie set from the nineteen fifties.

Pristine forests showed themselves on one side of the island offering a lush green view of nature, but on the leeward side an incredible wall of craggy rock surfaces could be found sulking miserably. These resembled the buttressed walls of a hundred grotesque cathedrals standing erect and stoic, awaiting their Quasi Modo to ring the bells. No one in his right mind would dare explore the deep caves hidden in the mixed terrain, especially because the pounding surf eddied in and out of the high boulders at water level penetrating well into dreary mysterious cracks. Seldom examined by humans, it was the unfriendliest place on the island. The water that touched these forboding bastions of bedrock ran deep, very deep, right up to the rockface and far enough within to hide the bones of any curious climber. Though rare, a life was sometimes lost there.

The nation of Timano began its birthing pains in the latter part of 1944, when some members of the Imperial Japanese Navy had been assigned to occupy it and keep it for Japan.

It was an ideal fortress owing mostly to the high rock surface and height advantage one would have on the plateau where the village was actually located. No superpower of the forties would have bothered bombing such an insignificant target. The docking area was situated at the only fold in the land which would allow a small harbor. After debarking, visitors would have to climb rather steep trails, about three hundred feet, to the plateau. This fact alone seemed to keep people away, but once on the high land everything was beautiful, like a Pacific Shangri-La. The raging surf was left to itself, a far drop below.

It didn't take the Japanese navy observers long to realize that no one was coming here. It was just what they wanted. No outsider could stand the isolation for long except the brave teachers. Keeping the island's big secret would be no problem; a fact Naoki hated. None of the teachers ever got a hint of what was really there. And it was a very, very old secret.

*Alan De Wolfe*

After the Japanese men had been on Timano awhile, they began to get comfortable with their new-found paradise soon marrying into the peaceful native tribe they'd surprised with their presence. True to the nature of civilizations of the southern Pacific they were welcomed, for they were good men, not the monsters the world's press made them out to be. The Japanese newcomers soon realized they had been conquered by innocence. The men, weary of battle and not willing to go home, wouldn't have cared anyway. Their allegiance to the emperor had become a moot point. To a man, they fell in love with the island and resided here in ecstasy for the next few decades. They had been happy to be far removed from the rigors of the failing Imperial Navy.

The children of these disenfranchised sailors were a breathtaking mix of Polynesian and Japanese and were known on neighboring islands as being very beautiful. The islands nearest Timano were close enough, but not too close, with very few having any population. All had the same high rockface-and-plateau look about them and by the lay of the land were unfriendly ports to say the least. The few islands having any population at all were not nearly as close as the others. But somehow love, being what it is, found a way for some of Naoki's friends to visit the other islands and marry, eventually returning to the patch of earth they'd known since childhood. Naoki scrupulously avoided marriage hoping one day to travel to the U.S. and study. However, time was running out for him. Thirty-two was old and he knew it.

"Father, what can I do to change your mind?"

Naoki's father was not unkind. "Perhaps someday the time will be right, son. You must trust me."

The government of elders was set up on Timano soon after the Japanese "castaways" arrived. The island people interacted with the outside world only enough to trade for what their tiny population needed. Sugar cane and pineapples grew well in the bright tropical sun blazing relentlessly down on them and provided a modest income for all citizens. The most respected

*Attack of the Koto Maru*

elder was Naoki's father, who just at this moment gave his final "no" to his son's demand.

"It cannot be ignored forever!" Naoki shouted after his father. The elder signaled the end of the conversation by walking away. "I will do something about this!" the young man steamed. "I swear it!" Naoki drew back, gave up for now, and lit his cooking fire. It was the angriest he'd ever been in his entire life.

## CHAPTER FOUR

Susan jumped up in sheer fright as an unloading tackle hit the side of the container. Despite her groggy state, she dragged herself quickly to the opening she'd peered from earlier and took a slanted look below. The ship was not moving. In fact, it was moored solidly to strong pilings. Had she slept that soundly?

The vista beyond showed a promontory jutting out into the ocean with beautiful but tangled vegetation and lovely dark beaches. The sand ran all the way up to the raised parking lot and was drab brown, some of it black like volcanic sand. "Oh, God, what now?" she wondered with hazy focus. "It looks like morning." It was time to muster her resolve.

The work crew clambered all around her steel prison attaching various cables for off-loading and positioning via the enormous deck crane. Ranar bellowed, "That one, put it here, do it now!" His polished English struck her with mild surprise. The only plan she could think of came charging forward into desperate focus. Her mouth said quietly, "Man, I hope this works."

The crane whirred and clanked prior to hookup handily maneuvered by three hardworking men huffing and puffing and perspiring. Susan caught their heavy scent as their close proximity served to frighten her more. Someone yelled in thickly accented English.

"Okay, it is ready!"

In a moment she felt a jolt as the container's weight caused the lifting cables to hum tight. The deck crane labored hard to move the two-ton container slowly from its tie-downs to a height of about forty feet, a fact which shot a feeling of terror through Susan still observing from her only lookout point. Bad as it was, her view from the container was magnificent, showing a long coastline, a house of polished beauty and an interminable fortress-like wall jutting out from a grassy highland. The entire situation seemed unreal to a girl whose upbringing never prepared her for people of true evil. She positioned herself according to her plan and awaited with dread the opening of the container door.

Meanwhile in Washington, Mark Ingram made the happy discovery that a friend of his in the Air Force was going to be right where he wanted him today. Admiral Jessup remained strangely on his mind as he completed his phone call, but he'd begun to get a feeling of optimism.

"Hello Jerry?"

"Yes, who's this? Mark?"

"Yeah. Say old pal, I understand you're going up today."

Jerry shunted the phone to his other ear. "Well, yes. Why do you ask?"

"Any chance you'll be hitting quadrants three and seven?"

Jerry frowned a little and chastened his friend. "Now Lieutenant Ingram, you know that's classified."

Mark stiffened enough to let Jerry know he was serious. "I need level-two pictures of those Pacific quadrants very much. How about it?"

The SR-71 pilot answered with a tinge of remorse. "What makes you think I take pictures anymore? You know they've retired all Blackbirds, except mine. Sorry, I can't do it." Then he added, "When do you want them?"

Mark smiled at Jerry's invective. His curiosity gained momentum when he remembered an admiral, his boss, who didn't seem trustworthy anymore, if he ever was. His long-standing mistrust of Jessup was usually dismissed with apathetic platitudes, but the intentional hedging and out-and-out and lying about his staff had lately made Mark especially watchful. "How dumb does he think I am?" Mark glowered.

His instincts had sharpened beyond his desire to subdue them owing to many months of watching Jessup's political maneuvering. The common denominator in Washington is money and power and the ability to use people to one's advantage. Even if Jessup was exonerated a few years back in the President Nixon scandals, Mark never really trusted him after that. His devious nature always seemed to be lurking in the background.

He popped his mind back to the matter at hand and sent a smile to his friend Jerry through the phone line. "Is tomorrow too soon?"

Jerry laughed, hung up the phone and carried on with his day, completely oblivious to the danger felt by a Pentagon secretary halfway round the world, on an island the high-flying pilot would soon have in his camera sights - literally.

On Catena Island, the container Susan was occupying frightened nearly to death now rested in the middle of an off-loading lot flat on the ground. The sun was bright and very hot, the air-conditioning had stopped. Outside the rusted box, a tanned and hot Ranar Moolong felt a trickle of sweat run from his forehead. "Open it!"

Two men, one on either side of the top surface pulled the locking pins at exactly the same time. The front side, hinged at the bottom pivoted just a crack then roared to the ground with a resounding thud. It covered the sound of a car's starting motor. Ranar wondered what he'd heard.

With the Ferrari in first gear, Susan gave him no time to think when he peered into the dark box. She screamed the car's wheels against the floor of the metal container causing it to snake wildly out into the light of day. It leaped gracefully but resolutely past its horrified owner, pebbles and dust from its undercarriage blasting backwards into the cavernous container. The debris pelted its staccato melody against the rust-red metal of the container and against the surprised faces of the crew. A blue smokey smell of Pirelli rubber singed the nostrils of the deck workers as the car's owner yelled, "After her!"

The men headed for various conveyances knowing she couldn't get far, for this was after all, an island. It bolstered his confident feeling that eventually he and his men would win. Ranar watched her spin round in the large dirt lot and said with eyes aflame, "I like a girl with spunk!"

*Attack of the Koto Maru*

Every way a sun-blinded Susan chose to go was blocked with insurmountable barriers. Workers scattered haphazardly out of her path when the squinting woman sent clouds of dust billowing high into the lazy afternoon.

The gleaming red sportster provided a throatful of dust for everyone including Susan. Her heart thumped ferociously within a heaving chest. The car continued to do parking lot "donuts" as the driver sought desperately for a way out of the borderless prison. Ranar was intrigued watching the commotion hoping very much that his car would be returned intact. He winced each time she nearly hit something. An inspired Susan finally exited onto the coast road and proceeded through all four remaining gears to put a great yawning gap between herself and the pursuers. She found a moment of relief knowing she was underway and leaving her wicked captors behind.

Two or three miles down the beach the sounds of screaming tires were heard by the beachcombing Paul Stevens.

"Judas Priest. What's that?"

Sheilding his eyes from the bright day he observed a small red dot in the distance gaining speed along the beach road. It danced in and out of sight amidst the deep green tropical growth overhanging some areas and gone from others. The "boxer" engine exuded a familiar sound gaining speed effortlessly in his vision and reminding him of his own Ferrari, now a remote memory.

Paul continued to dig, but with one eye on the road. "Humph, whoever owns the island forgot the speed limit signs." He offered only a casual acknowledgement of the speeding car, again, not wishing to agitate any suspicions. His hat found its way back to his head and was cocked downward to further hide his eyes.

Susan could hear her pursuers screeching around behind her, but knew that the car she was commanding could get away from the devil himself if called upon to do so. It helped her relax a bit and put time and distance between them. The tank was full, visibility was good and with her own confidence improving, it seemed she would get away after all. She'd show them. If she could get back to civilization, she'd sue somebody for something.

The secretary from Cincinnati had no idea that perhaps the road was little more than a ring around an island and that soon she'd be "in a pickle", as her mom might say. The coast road was just that and circumscribed the island in a most predictable way.

"If I can only find a hotel or something. With a nice road like this there must be some resorts nearby."

Susan mouthed her innocent words careening past Paul in unbridled fury, trailing steamy smoke and unmuffled sounds behind, throttling down for the curve. She briefly noticed him out on the beach collecting drift-worthy prizes. The sight of him validated her notion that the coastline must have resorts and hotels nearby. Her mood improved.

Shortly behind the rushing red car came the thunderous roar of five pursuing vehicles. Their comparatively slow speeds showed that the drivers wished to err on the side of caution lest they overturn on the unbanked curve near the American beachcomber. Experience hinted to Paul that the first car was being chased, though the why of it was not apparent. Knowing there was more to come in this drama, he proceeded to slink up through the hedgerow used for last night's undercover excursion and let himself fade momentarily from the constant sweep of snooping cameras. The electronic eyes appeared to be watching the roadway, though from that distance he couldn't tell for sure.

After about six miles of fast driving Susan saw something ahead. "Oh no!" she said aloud. "It's that damned parking lot where I started! All I've seen is water on my right! This must be a friggin' island!" Susan knew that in times past, when her vocabulary sank to the level of modern vernacular her situation had always proven serious. Anxiety rose in her like a World Trade Center elevator.

Her kidnapper had thrown out a roadblock just before the off-loading area which was spread well across the roadway. But the indefatigable Susan decided this barrier would have to be

*Attack of the Koto Maru*

compromised too. Her heart quickened and her eyes searched wildly for salvation. The shift knob vibrated under her right hand. Decision time had arrived.

She neared the blockade going far too fast for comfort, which was a fact that produced a fast-dawning worry on Ranar's face. With eyes enlarging bigger and bigger as the last moments came, he told himself, "Surely she will not try to breach this line of vehicles!"

As one could imagine, the speed of the car gave the driver a visual array descending in perspective like one of Salvadore Dali's phantasmagoric paintings. In spite of it, Susan suddenly saw her deliverance to the right of the roadblock and hit the throttle. After an ominous downshift Ranar saw her coming straight for him and yelled, "No, no, no!"

She veered right at the last practical moment forcing the car off the road, up a steep mound and into the open air above. The unrehearsed flight accomplished her objective with remarkable ferocity. The car just barely made it to the sandy apron of the raised off-loading lot and remained tilted in soft sand.

Stuck momentarily on the mushy perimeter and disappointed to be back where she started, the frantic secretary stood on the accelerator and sent a biting hail of sand off the high edge into Ranar's face. It filled the clothes of the island's infuriated owner with gritty discomfort. He found a moment to launch a string of foreign expletives. Unfortunately for the racing young Pentagon worker, his mood changed.

Then the low-slung Ferrari sprang forward into the same lot which held the rusty sea container and slowed miraculously to a spinning, screaming halt. In the dust swirling above and around the car, the woman collected herself, revved the engine again and shot out onto the same coast road fighting back desperate tears. It was deja vu she could have lived without.

Once again Paul heard the mystifying sounds of the boiling conflagration traveling water-borne all the way from what seemed to be the island's loading area. He remained crouched in the bushes and watched the gum chewing heavies who had chased the red car, double back from the other direction until they were at the curve roughly in front of him. "What on earth is going on?" He laid low with his thoughts while the men blocked the road in anticipation of stopping whoever was in the sprinting Ferrari.

In only a moment's time the speedy Italian "omologato" reappeared from the distance going full tilt again. When it neared the curve in front of Paul the driver saw the roadblock far too late to slow down. This time her abrupt change of direction would give her only air and sky to view through the windshield.

Susan hit the brakes quickly, but it was only a token attempt. Her once-saving automobile suddenly became an airborne projectile flying gracefully and in seeming slow motion off the end of the island fast enough for takeoff, but sadly lacking in airfoil surface and sustained thrust. The Ferrari's end-against-end weight ratio became an important factor in Susan's survival, for the car crashed flat in the water skipping like a stone thrown by a fisherboy. It came slowly to a stop and sank about a foot into the calm shallow surface.

The brakes on Ranar's Land Rover sang a symphony of dissonant squeals as he drew up to the scene fuming in anger. Grit still clung to the perspiration of his neck and chest.

"Excellency, your car is sinking!" one man exclaimed.

"I know, you idiot! Bring her to me!" he ordered, stepping down in lengthy stride.

"Her?" Paul thought. "Excellency? Is this guy royalty?" From his covert viewing spot he saw Susan and mumbled, "It's a woman?" The bush jiggled as its visitor shifted around for a better view.

After a few impatient minutes, the men struggled to bring the neatly hogtied Susan face to face with her captor. She splashed ashore writhing in the clutches of her captors and shouted with vigor, "You sleazy, scum-sucking banana republic jackass! Who gave you the power to kidnap innocent people!"

"Innocent? Oh hardly, Ms. Black. You have seen too much on that little report of yours about my nuclear...well, never mind. I'm afraid you can't go back, at least, not alive."

"But it wasn't my report! I was delivering it! I never saw..."

Susan writhed again, kicking the man restraining her where no man wants to be kicked causing him to relax his grip and cry out. "Take her to the house!" came the order.

Once again the men brought her twisting body under control. She tried one last time, exclaiming, "But I don't know anything about your stupid business!"

Neither, it seemed, did a wide-eyed Paul Stevens, sitting secretly in the jungle shrubs. "The thought of this obviously-rich heathen having a nuclear _anything_ just ruins the hell outta my day!" Paul sighed, knowing that some independent, slightly paunchy, well tanned beachcomber was probably going to have to take another nocturnal hike and do something about it.

## CHAPTER FIVE

Throughout the years crafters of prose and poetry have been able to save entire manuscripts by adding a moonlight rendezvous or two to a story of dubious quality. Lovers have always had unlimited fodder for romance and elopements 'neath the mystical haloed moon and sensual paintings of evening scenes draped with hanging mists have usually been enormously enhanced when the artist merely adds moonlight. Such things impart a cozy ambiance to all who read it, view it or feel it.

On the other hand, the haunting fright of being alone and walking on a rural road at night with no flashlight or beacon of any kind requires a splash of high-resolution moonlight to coax the ugly phantom of all things evil from the shadows. Out they spring from the bushes to chase the hiker through dimly lit open areas, with twisted apparitions and imaginary dangers born of his own illogic, leaving him to view moonlight without the same comfort level known only moments before.

It was with profound trepidation that Paul walked along the deserted coast road that evening, his body bathed now and again in the silver gleam of moonbeams. The eerie luminescence played off some of the hairs of his head - the gray ones - and spilt down over his shoulders casting a tenuous shadow on the macadam under him. It heightened his worry about some of the possible animal inhabitants of this lush tropical paradise. Back where his campfire was sizzling away, a bag of beans stood propped in silhouette on a beach chair with the old hat he'd got in Australia on top. "Hope the cameras can't tell the difference," he muttered.

The tropical noises were always frightening to him, especially tonight, but he resolutely kept inching his way toward the docks and toward the possible rescue of the mystery girl he'd seen earlier. Who was she? By her language he supposed she was American. And what did she mean by "banana republic jackass? And kidnapped? Oh, Gawd!

*Attack of the Koto Maru*

At a point near the docking area the coast road passed by the long drive to the house above. The owner had great faith in his electronic snooping system and Paul was glad to see hardly any security at all of the human type. The snooping gear appeared to be shut off, a fortuitous by-product of princely arrogance, and he hoped it bode well for his covert mission. His excess saliva sounded like two rocks rubbing one another when he swallowed.

Ascending the road from the waterfront with great stealth, he soon approached the multi-level house which was, indeed, a centerpiece in a splendid island setting. It was spacious and rambling in architecture, a sort of split level hacienda with courtyards and terraces sprinkled about, softly lit with subtle illuminations strong in his vision on the high walls. Cornerstones of the western wall showed through the branches of tropical growth hiding him as he stalked closer. This house he had seen from a distance was now within touch. His pulse quickened.

He stepped out from dense cover to a walkway which ringed the house where, he supposed, a scheming rich person might stroll to formulate some insidious plan. Paul sneaked without a sound along the terrace wall orienting himself carefully for eventual escape.

From his position just below the rim of the terrace floor, he ducked as Ranar give a loud order. "Freddie, bring a cigar!"

His back firmly against the wall, Paul noticed that the moonlight had returned to looking beautiful again from the silly mind-bending effects of a few minutes ago. Though a little too bright for sneaking around, the moon's cool light defined the edge of the terrace walls and blended with soft lights from the house.

Bathed in pale illuminations, Ranar received a cigar from his right-hand man. The odd little man with warts in profusion about his neck and face kindled the cigar in his own mouth until it glowed evenly across the surface. The principle bad guy then took it, puffed it and turned it to assure a perfect light. Freddie's smile caused his warty face to present some of his blemishes higher than others.  His tragic skin condition helped make his comical countenance less laughable.  Paul mused entirely within his own mind.  "Gawd, he looks like Smiley Burnett, and I certainly wouldn't want him sucking on *my* cigar!"

"Thank you, Freddie.  Did the admiral call?"

Freddie replied to the question with a feminine lisp.  "Not today, thurr."

Surprised by the moist, effeminate little voice, Paul turned round and stifled a giggly laugh somewhere in his hands and shirt.  The man appeared to have all the base characteristics of a simian anthropoid but combined them hysterically with the flip motions of a drag queen.  The chuckling interloper below the wall finally overcame his spot of humor not a moment too soon.  A woman's voice startled him back to reality.

"Alright, alright!  Take your hands off me!"

Susan strode in with her lovely shape vibrating.  Her feet beat heavily on her shoe treads tapping hastily across the squares of terra cotta.  "So what now, hot shot?"

Paul thought, "Yep, she's American."

Her captor appreciated her good looks using a sustained leer to accentuate it.  In a silky day dress she had swirled to a stop in the middle of the terrace.  The dress looked like a madras plaid puffball pinched at the waist by a small cloth belt.  Her lace-up walking shoes seemed to go well with the outfit albeit totally unplanned.  The smiling Ranar answered Paul's nagging question regarding her identity.  "Come now, Susan Black.  Why not be friendlier?"

"Listen Radar, or whatever your name is.  My mother always told me to avoid snakes.  You're a good-looking guy but you're doing it all wrong - you know, with five wives or so.  What's the matter with these goofball women?"

"But it is our way.  Why fight it?  You're here on Catena until we eventually go back to my kingdom, which is in another part of this great ocean.  I'm not the sultan yet, but my father is very old.  Who can say what might happen?  Enjoy your stay!  We will leave after my very special business is concluded."

Ranar rose to leave and said, "Freddie will bring you some food here to the veranda." He then turned to Susan. "We will have a marriage ceremony in a few days. You must be fit and ready for our consummation."

Susan watched him exit and was left in a speechless, wide-eyed gape. Her mouth remained open as she collapsed into a seat along the wall. "Oh no," she said very quietly. "Consummation. This guy's gonna marry me!"

Paul heard her utterance at the same moment he realized who the future sultan was. Back in his own dreary days of investing other people's money, he remembered that Ranar Moolong had begun to get a blacksheep reputation of epic proportion. No broker trusted the wayward prince, but the Pacific bad boy had to be endured because of his ungodly amounts of capital. Paul said without sound, "Boy, I wish I was in a Manhattan coffee shop right now."

The dazed woman sat near a low spot on the courtyard's raised platform looking blankly off the edge, down the hill and into the harbor's night time reflectance. A crouching Paul peeled his backside off the wall and came into focus just below her elbow. The terrace light flashed across his face.

"Oh!" she exclaimed.

"Shh..." Paul asserted, exaggerating his whisper. "How many people are in the immediate area?"

Susan looked around to see nothing and no one. "Everyone is off doing something. Oh! Some guy is heading this way to fatten me up!" She noted the imminent arrival of Freddie with evening food. Without even knowing Paul, something about his presence spelled relief in her mind.

"Listen. After he walks away, swing your legs out off the edge and jump. I'll be here below to help you." Paul's whispered advice relieved Susan.

"Who are you?"

Paul inserted finality into his voice when he offered an unforgettable truth. "I'm your only way off this island."

*Alan De Wolfe*

Coincidental to the furtive conversation on the island of Catena, back in Washington, D.C. dawn broke into a sunny day and Lieutenant Mark Ingram was on his door step accepting a courier package. He dashed to his shop fiddling with the flaps of the slim package which he opened as he walked.

"Boy, that was fast. Good old Jerry. Now we'll see if I'm thinking correctly."

The lieutenant quickly popped open an inside envelope and began probing the photos. The light in his workshop was exceptionally strong for a good reason - he had been involved in the reconnaissance effort during the war in the Persian Gulf and some of that work he'd done at home. He knew the value of strong light and knew just what to look for regarding spy photos. Some of the exposures were high-grain photos and some were infrared shots. All were very interesting.

A magnified examination of the quadrant three area he was most interested in brought forth a penetrating look at a group of islands in an eighty-mile chain. Some were uninhabited, some were private and some were nations by themselves. "What nice shots!" Mark spoke to himself adjusting his electronic lupe and peering at every detail.

The film zipped under his gaze in the way a book store clerk might check his microfiche, though this film was infinitely more interesting. Abruptly Catena slid beneath his view. "What's this?"

Staring again through his lupe he noticed an island with a big rectangle almost covering it. "It's gotta be a building. Wow! It's big! And look at the center - open to the sky. Good thing the blackbirds fly high."

The puzzled viewer knew for sure that such a thing had to cost a king's ransom in those climes. Little could be seen inside the open rectangle for it was a photo snapped from about thirty thousand feet, but he sensed he was on to something. Who could afford such a thing? Someone of royalty, perhaps?

*Attack of the Koto Maru*

"Well, well," he said calmly, squinting further. "Ranar Moolong, I think I've found you. What a slippery rascal you are!"

Mark stood militarily erect and gave his pilot friend Jerry a private salute, "My hat's off to you, old pal!" then sank into a chair to compose his plan for the next few days. "Somehow I've gotta get to the middle of the Pacific Ocean!" Far and away, he knew that the most difficult part of his situation would come soon, in the morning to be exact. A sleeping pill exploded later in his stomach after the evening news but left him in fitful sleep. It was the only way an excited Mark Ingram would be able to sleep at all on this night of revelation.

When 8:00 A.M. rolled around the next day, he shaved, showered and took the beltway to work as always. Before long, he stood outside the big oak door and prepared himself for a conference with the Rear Admiral.

"Jeez...what if he says no?" He rapped on Jessup's door and shined his shoes with the back of his pantlegs. "Well, I have to try."

"Good morning Admiral Jessup," Mark stepped in and saluted.

"Good morning, Ingram." Jessup barely looked up from his papers. "What did you want to see me about?"

"Ah, well sir," Mark fumbled for words, "It's been about four years since I had a vacation, sir, and if it's all right with you..."

"By all means, lieutenant!" the man roared. "Get yourself outta here and relax in some exotic place. Give your work to someone else, you've earned it!" Jessup felt immediate relief knowing that the only person who could figure out his nefarious scheme might now be safely away on vacation. Mark stood dumbfounded.

"Go ahead and use anything the navy has to get you where you decide to go. I'll give you authorization, it'll be on your desk in an hour."

"Thank you, sir!"

*Alan De Wolfe*

The surprised lieutenant snapped off a parting salute and got out, lest the admiral change his mind. Standing stunned a fraction of a minute later outside the admiral's door, he still couldn't believe his ears. "Holy cow!" His mouth remained open. "That was effortless." In his mind, he knew he enunciated his request convincingly to the admiral, but in his heart, all his instincts told him it had been a little too easy.

But this was not the time to dwell on some useless supposition. Deep thought ceased to be necessary and that was that, there were other things to do. He shook Jessup out of his head and let plans take the place of curiosity in a mind whizzing and buzzing about how to accomodate his need. The newly-freed lieutenant had to get to the middle of the Pacific Ocean in a relatively short time and had the entire navy at his disposal. To Mark, it didn't seem reasonable, given the admiral's cheery frame of mind, that he would be denied a month, or even more, to traipse around in hopes of finding something concrete regarding Ranar Moolong, crown prince of Malua. Even though the admiral didn't know exactly what he was up to, the proper authorizations would come in handy when pulling the necessary strings for equipment. One of the pieces of equipment was an item he hadn't used for quite some time. Something with wings. The review would be fun.

A navy man always knows where his ships are. He considered the Pacific theater and, playing with his words, thought, "Maybe Uncle <u>Nimitz</u> wouldn't mind having me around for a while."

Back down the hall, Jessup picked up the phone to call one of the three men who were in on his plan. In his thirty-two years as a navy man he couldn't remember feeling more relieved, for he too had been worried about the very thorough Mark Ingram.

Ingram was the kind of lieutenant every member of high-ranking brass considered indispensable. Nothing got past Mark, especially something with a little mystery attached to it. He had to know it all, no matter how minute the smallest detail, no matter how many feet would be stepped on. Jessup knew he'd been trained well by his father, also a navy man and was happy to give him some time off. Now, with the lieutenant heading for vacation everything would go smoothly and everyone would be relieved. His lieutenant's reputation for thoroughness wouldn't matter in a few days. He and his consorts would be aboard the old BALBOA, making their way toward the southern Pacific and toward the one thing that drives the dreams of most men - money. The navy officer sat back, completed his call, and made the mistake of dismissing Mark Ingram too quickly from his thoughts.

## CHAPTER SIX

On Timano, Naoki decided to turn in early this evening and not go with his friends for one of their long talk sessions. He had nearly given up ever convincing his father to bring the island into the modern world. "All he wants to do is go to the cut and work, work, work. And what for?" He repeated as he had so many times before, "And I can't stand one more minute of the drills!" He sat back and considered turning in.

Without warning, a vibrating thud happened all around him! He fell to the ground instinctively, relieved to find it had dissipated after only a second or two.

"Earthquake!" he shouted with no good reason. Who could he warn? All on the island had felt it. In fact, people in the entire chain of islands had felt it in varying degrees including those on Catena. It was over almost instantly, becoming nothing more than a seismic statistic in the history of his volcanic islands. Naoki heaved a deep sigh and lost his concern, but eighty miles north, the steno from the Pentagon nearly jumped out of her shoes. Susan watched Paul lose his footing down the steep embankment.

"What was that?

"Earthquake!" he said affrighted. "Jeez, that's all we need! Why does trouble come in buckets? Come on. Now that you're outta that house, keep moving!"

At the big house on the plateau no one had yet noticed the disappearance of Ranar's special guest, but everyone felt the ground disturbance. The whereabouts of a "guest" was not much of a concern anyway because on an island, one's imprisonment is controlled by the water's eternal presence. A person could go nowhere.

"There, down through this hedgerow and we're nearly there."

The two Americans with escape on their minds ran with frantic step along the remainder of the coast road then off into the row of bushes leading to the water's edge.

"Oww!" Susan cried.

"Oh, sorry. I should have told you about these nettles." Paul hoped Susan wouldn't be missed for at least another half hour. They quickly reached the lower end of the hedgerow.

"Okay, stay here under cover. I'm going to crouch along the beach and hope I can get to my campsite without being spotted. Then I'll work my way into my beach chair and pretend to get up and stretch. After that I'll walk back here like I'm taking a walk."

Susan asked, "How will I get to the boat?"

"That's the hard part. You'll have to walk on the other side of me, away from the cameras and match my stride carefully. We will imprint their sensing devices as one person, I hope."

"So do I," Susan gulped.

Paul skittered quickly away on this three-quarter moon night remembering the earth shocks of a moment ago and vaguely aware that seismic sea waves (tsunami) result from all quakes which happen at sea. From extensive reading he knew the waves could be anything from barely noticeable to three hundred feet high. "Could be," he thought, "the comparatively slight temblor tonight won't raise the waves very high. It's the wrong kind of harbor for tsunamis anyway."

Paul did just as he said, returning in a short time for Susan. They walked back to the camp sticking close together and showing the cameras one person - they hoped. They needn't have bothered. The lazy guards were not watching the monitors very closely.

"I guess I'm correct about the water."

"What do you mean?" Susan inquired.

"I think there will be no tsunami here. This evening's waves are only a foot or two, maybe less. Kinda calm."

"You mean tidal waves?"

"Well, that name is incorrect. There are no such things as 'tidal waves'. Tsunamis are the proper name and are caused by seismic events. You just have to hope you're not where they are!"

The two of them continued their close walk huffing and puffing as he filled Susan in on the strength of big waves. He felt a little more comfortable falling into scholarly chatter.

"It remains, however, that unless one is familiar with the local topography it's never wise to ignore undersea earthquakes. See this little harbor? If it were V-shaped instead of flat as you see it, we might have had large waves. It's a relief to see the water calm." Paul kept talking to diffuse Susan's anxiety.

"This island doesn't have the V-shaped harbors necessary to heighten the sea swells to the monstrous waves of legend. During the moment before tsunamis occur, waters near shore rush suddenly outward leaving all harbored ships to wallow in the mud of the harbor floor. Then in a few minutes, the water comes roaring back with a vengeance, accumulating disastrously within a V-shaped harbor."

"If the harbor has a sharply ascending sea floor, it causes the water to build on itself and climb to nightmarish heights, decreasing in speed from up to six hundred mph at sea to about fifty mph at landfall. As the lower water decreases in speed, the trillions of gallons behind it pile into and over the slower water resulting in a towering wall of water ranging from twenty to three hundred feet in height! They are not usually witnessed by anyone, because no one lives through it. Fortunately they are rare happenings."

"Thank heaven!"

Paul added in portent, "Of course, earthquakes usually come in groups."

Shortly after Paul's verbal essay, the two walkers arrived at his camp on the beach. Susan got herself in front of a big bundle Paul was about to carry to his boat. He walked out into the water holding the bundle with the woman in front, concealed, and pushed her along with its canvas material. The guards noticed Paul's action and discussed his departure from the island in lazy repartee. To them nothing seemed out of the ordinary. The American was leaving, so what. At the boat, Susan slipped over

*Attack of the Koto Maru*

the rail undetected and headed for the cabin downstairs in the hull. Paul's whisper was moderately loud.

"I'm going back for the rest of my stuff, then in a few minutes we'll push off. Don't turn the light on yet in the cabin."

Paul hated to shove off at night because of impenetrable blackness, but the moon was quite bright tonight and the weather for the next few days was supposed to be perfect. He was just glad to have fooled them all and very glad the girl was safe. In his mind he was plotting a course in front of one island and behind the next all the way to the distant Timano in case they were pursued. This head start is all they would need.

He gathered the rest of his gear, untied the skiff and walked the rope out into the water. The hull slid without sound from the soft sands of Catena to the deeper black of the ocean. The last grains of sand washed cleanly from his feet when he jumped his butt up onto the varnished slick of the dark brown decking. Soft music came from below indicating Susan had found the tape player.

After boarding, he gathered the ropes and made his way to the upper cabin. In a moment his small engine started. The sea had become dead calm. They were off and running.

"No sail tonight," the beachcomber said aloud, setting his throttle at an easy fifteen knots. "Not that I would, anyway." His guest brought her pleasing form deckside and sat near the wheel. At last he had a moment to get to know her.

"Susan, tell me how you got into this mess."

Susan laid herself back against the deck cushions to bask in the balmy breezes. She liked Paul but had a private feeling that he'd been alone too long on the heaving swells of the southern Pacific. His salt and pepper hair framed his craggy yet handsome face as a person might well expect of a grizzled explorer. The idea of living completely without another interacting soul seemed odd to her, but she could easily imagine in this wonderful moonlight why it might be appealing. She easily told him her brief story right up to the minute, and ended it with, "So you see, I never did know that this jerk with many wives was building a bomb! He thought I knew all about it, or maybe his henchmen thought so. They talked openly about it when they were manhandling me after the Ferrari hit the lagoon. Anyway, they swiped me right off the Washington Beltway, do you believe the nerve?"

A dawning broke through into Paul's conscious. "A bomb! Of course! I knew I'd seen that configuration before. Those were the small 'machines' I saw them working on in the big bunker. Wow!"

"You mean, you saw them?"

"Yes! Oh, man! Somebody's got big trouble. I don't imagine he's going to use them himself - prob'ly sell them to some misanthrope."

Paul noticed Susan's obvious fatigue. "Sorry you spent all that time in the container. It must have been awful."

"It was! But I had a heck of a romp in a Ferrari!"

Paul was amused at her smile, then showed puzzlement. "These days with the world at peace, well, sort of, I wonder who'd buy a doomsday bomb? The North Koreans? The Iranians? The Libyans?"

"Ha! World at peace indeed!," the woman butt-in. "A person wouldn't have to look far to find a powderkeg of some kind. You should work at the Pentagon if you want to know about powderkegs!"

"No thanks! You can have it. I've done my time as a handler of other people's money and that has its dangers too."

She continued, "Like you, I have no idea who'd want nuclear devices, but we've got to get to a place with a telephone. I have a few connected friends in Washington and they'll get something done about it. I've got to call someone. Maybe, Admiral Jessup."

Paul, though he considered himself an old fogey, appreciated the soft beauty of the Cincinnati beauty in the soft light of the deck lounge. "We'll head for the island of Timano. It has more of the modern conveniences plus I've heard the people are wonderful. It's about eighty miles. I've never actually landed

*Attack of the Koto Maru*

there but I think it's high time. Settle back and get some sleep. At dawn I'll be hoisting the sail."

"I can't sleep. This much water gives me the creeps."

"Well, try to rest. We may actually get away with this if we get enough of a head start," Paul smiled to comfort her.

Susan's uncertain mood was perhaps typical of a social person who had been rudely cut-off from other human beings then suddenly reconnected. "I don't know why he put me in a container. He owns the entire ship and everyone on it. How far could I have swam?"

Paul added, "Some perverse misuse of power, maybe?"

"He could just be a rat. I'm glad it's over."

"We're not in the clear yet."

Usually a scene on a skiff under scintillating moonlight, paints a calm romantic picture but not tonight, as they both felt the urgency of becoming far removed from this particular area. Paul still wasn't sure they could get far enough away and feared new rumblings from the earth's shifting tectonic plates.

The duo's new friendship, however, grew with each word during their first hour at sea. The engrossing conversations tended to snuff out their caution. Each talked at length and paid no attention to a slight hum that matched the hum of Paul's own engines.

In what seemed like only a moment, Ranar's craft appeared suddenly across their bows. The quietness of their power boat shocked Paul.

"Thstop where you are!" an effeminate voice called out in a roar of reversing engines. The two new friends looked at each other with the same sinking sensation.

"Uh oh...I know who that is!"

Paul killed the engine. Some of Freddie's seamen jumped aboard the skiff's bow as it came to a rest dead in the water. Their steps rocked his boat leaving him to hit his ships wheel in angst knowing the escape had been for naught. He watched with pained expression when the boats bumped together, and he knew their escape course would now be reversed. The malefactors fed a rope through the deck's front eye bracket and secured Paul's smaller boat for the short journey back to Catena. No master of any boat likes to enter port under tow. Paul felt his anger rise. All he could do was look at Susan's sad face and fight back his own regrets.

In under an hour, the two unfortunate captives sat once again in the patio area of the main house on Catena thinking back on their negated escape plan.

"Sorry it didn't work, Susan."

"I must be jinxed. Now I've got you in trouble."

"Don't worry about that," he said, watching the confident Ranar walk in. Paul planned anew, listening to Ranar Moolong speak with calm assurance.

"Mr. Stevens, did you really think you'd get away so easily? It amused me to watch the whole thing unfold once we discovered the girl missing. Freddie is a very suspicious person. He knew very quickly something was not right." From across the room Freddie smiled with a menace Paul had not noticed before. Susan sat in front of Paul who was standing and giving his own snarly look to Freddie.

"You see, it just made sense that you were somehow involved, especially when you pulled up anchor so soon after the woman's disappearance."

Paul demanded, "Just what are you doing with us anyhow. And what are you concealing here?"

His question was not important to the royal brat. "It does not concern you, Mr. Stevens. Anyway we are nearly finished." He turned to Susan and said, "Come here, my dear."

"Ha! I doubt it. Rats aren't my favorite vermin," she replied with disgust. Paul thought she shouldn't be quite that cocky.

Freddie, as if personally offended stormed over to her side, stiff-armed Paul to the floor and grabbed her mercilessly. "When the Mister Ranar thspeakths, you jump!"

The future potentate walked over and said, "Freddie, Freddie, take it easy." He looked lovingly at her, changed his expression slightly then laid a brutal slap across her face.

*Attack of the Koto Maru*

He roared, "Take them downstairs!" Susan and Paul were unceremoniously dragged off and thrown in two separate rooms adjacent to one another in a basement typical of the tropics - humid. Each slumped to the floor to compose themselves and wait for a spark of good old American ingenuity. Paul knew it would come. Just a matter of time.

Almost completely around the globe, Rear Admiral Jessup had no idea what had happened to the troublesome twosome as he was piped aboard the Balboa at that exact moment.

Ostensibly, the admiral had requested to be aboard his old command for its last voyage. The old cruiser had been sold to the Australian government for breaking up as scrap and Jessup wanted to ride her one last time, or so he said. On the way, the Balboa would make a slight joggle in its journey and drop the admiral and his pals off at some location convenient to the airlines. To anyone watching, it would seem like a short vacation on a nondescript island. Then later he would return home and get back to the usual drugery of the Pentagon, or at least, fake it. The Balboa had only twenty men, sufficient to run it to Melbourne for its final stop, afterwhich the navy men would be afforded a jet trip home. Admiral Jessup had asked three naval "friends" to join him which didn't appear unusual to Captain Conlin. The only cargo was a large box to be delivered with the admiral at his destination.

The ship was mastered by a Captain Tom Conlin, whom Jessup didn't even know. Captain Conlin hated to see the "old girl" go for scrap but the ravages of time had her on the run. The old battle wagon had always been a favorite of Admiral Jessup and he had many stories to tell of her valor during the Korean "police action", as Harry Truman called it. Now, she was little more than a collection of rust, armor plating and totally outdated technologies and secretly meant nothing to Jessup. From a distance she still looked awesome, and would have been, if she'd had any armament. The old tub carried enough fuel to get her to her destination plus a few thousand rounds of fifty millimeter cannon ammo only because it had been left near the guns by mistake. That was about all. At times, it seemed to the captain there was too much leakage in the plates for her to remain seaworthy, but somehow she did. The pumps ran twenty-four hours a day. He was concerned enough to specify that no more than a moderate eighteen knots be achieved during the voyage. The skeleton crew was instructed to "watch 'er good".

Admiral Jessup made sure she'd be alone and unescorted, but he didn't like the idea that they would have to cross the path of an old rival of his, a full admiral onboard the <u>Nimitz</u>. Jessup looked at the charting and muttered, "Jeez, why did that friggin' <u>Nimitz</u> have to have turbine trouble there?"

# CHAPTER SEVEN

"Ensign!"
"Yes sir, Admiral!"
"Any sign of Lieutenant Ingram yet?"
"No...oh, yes sir! He just came on radar."
The two navy men watched the Nimitz scanning screen. Mark flew his bird high and vertical, announcing his presence more quickly to the tactical radars of the aircraft carrier. The whine of the two Pratt & Whitney engines under his butt still felt good though he'd been in the air for over four hours. The old Phantom fighter was the only aircraft he was still checked out on, which is to say the only one he was qualified to deliver this day. Fortunately, the admiral aboard insisted on the required full complement of aircraft and the one Mark was driving would fill the list. He loved to fly but had enough hours only to fly the Phantom and was therefore stuck using them until he got some free time to absorb further instruction. Newer aircraft had passed beyond the old hardware long ago, but the old gas guzzlers were still a heck of a thrill to a pilot, and noisy as hell. He was sorry the flight hadn't lasted longer.

Below him in a light haze lay the Nimitz resting in a fifteen knot mode and enjoying a substantial headwind. It was a good landing day with the winds and ship's speed just right. The big beauty looked like a postage stamp on a huge blue mailing envelope when viewed from high above. Serious repairs were required for her main gearbox necessitating a full stop in mid-ocean for two hours at a time. The admiral had been heard to shout, "A ship should make way, not sit like an island!"

The big gray object wasn't sitting - exactly. Gearing repairs can require a two hour stop as one propeller is made to "trail" unpowered while the critical repair is carried out to its powerplant. It was just as the ship resumed headway that proper speed for landing was achieved. Mark's imprint had been spotted just a moment before. The ship was up and running but would have to stop again later.

Far above the flattop's decks the sea appeared calm as it does so often on the fringes of paradise. It surrounded the ship's silhouette with sun-sparkled water causing the vessel to look ghostly on its shimmering surface. It disappeared momentarily in the sun's blinding glare when Mark brought his fighter around into a steep bank. The speeding pilot flashed a matching glare off his wings into the eyes of the attending seamen on the flight deck and the crew of admiring men watched him scream one low pass over the flight deck to purposely splatter exhaust noise the length of the ship. It was a thing "the old man" didn't like.

His old engines crackled loudly and spit-out the marvelous noises loved by all men who sail aircraft carriers and caretake the planes. On his low pass Mark hit the afterburner and showed everyone including an admiral just stepping out on deck why <u>Phantoms</u> are so respected as acrobatic flyers. For the men, it was always a proud moment to watch one of their own boys handle the machinery they regarded so highly. The admiral shielded his eyes from the sun and muttered skyward.

"Damned hot dog!"

Roaring straight up in a climb, Mark forced the plane to do its best maneuvers twisting strongly forward into the blue Pacific morning and reaching thirty-thousand feet in no time. The men of the carrier stood exalted watching their flyboy, who had recently been asked to take some political, inglorious position in Washington go through his acrobatic regimen. Because his uncle wanted him to be in a safer area, Mark deferred graciously to his elder's wishes and left the <u>Nimitz</u> taking the stateside position in the Pentagon. He didn't care. He rather liked Washington. The dozens of cheering men who remembered him from times before missed him. His landing was welcomed by all aboard, but the re-engagement with his old messmates might be soured by the admiral's hot temper. He was soon standing in the admiral's quarters sweating out a lecture.

*Attack of the Koto Maru*

"Lieutenant Ingram, don't ever let me catch you hot-dogging in one of my planes again!

"Yes, Admiral sir!"

From behind his desk, the "old man" steamed, "If it wasn't necessary to have that unit back on the ship you never would have got back aboard. Whaddya think this is, a vacation?"

"Yes sir, Admiral Ingram! It is!"

The admiral looked straight into Mark's eyes and began a small smile. He reached out his arms and said warmly, "Nice flying, nephew."

Mark walked to his uncle and embraced him mightily. A few slaps on the back resonated off the walls of the admiral's rooms and Mark backed up to salute one more time. Admiral Ingram snapped off an acknowledgement then asked about Mark's mother, with genuine interest.

"How's my brother's beautiful bride?"

"As wonderful as ever, sir. You really ought to go back and marry her...sir."

The "old man" smiled, but quickly chided Mark with a reminder that his own brother, Mark's father, had died landing on a carrier in the Viet Nam action and told him not to get "too big for his britches".

"Thanks for bringing us the aircraft, Mark. I'll take that marriage thing under advisement. It was fortunate for us you wanted to come to this quadrant. We need the plane, and your old shipmates get a boost watching you. What are your plans on this big vacation of yours?"

Mark was hesitant to reveal the fact that he'd come to this area on a hunch and was going to see if he could get a look at the concrete structure on Catena.

"Well, I just want to relax a few days in these islands. Which one do you recommend?"

Without much thought Admiral Ingram said, "I'd take Timano. I hear only nice things about it. The people are very hospitable and always welcome new people though there's really nothing to do there except rent a boat and take a day trip - fish a little maybe. Bet it's good to get away from old Jessup, eh?"

"You said it! I hate to say it, but I have never trusted him."

"That might be why he never made full admiral. No one ever seems to know exactly what's on his mind. And I've never trusted him either."

"Well, while I'm here I want to forget Washington and do some serious sightseeing. If you don't mind sir, I'll have a chopper drop me off on the island tomorrow."

"Well...I suppose we could go over and pick up some fresh pineapple. I mean, I do have to justify a trip over." The admiral agreed to drop Mark off and added, "And we'll be back this way in about a week - if we ever get this overpriced metallic island running right. Then I have to get to a disarmament conference in Tokyo. They have radio-comm on Timano so I'll phone you about a day in advance of the ship's next pass." Admiral Ingram thought about his available aircraft and said, "Then we'll get you back to the mainland somehow."

After a good reunion with a man he admired so much, Mark walked out on deck in the morning sun to greet some of his old friends and past shipmates most of whom were just stepping out into the glorious Sunday sea air after shipboard services. God is important to a sailor. There is much peril on the sea, especially when the waves are high and no matter how big or modern the ship may be, harrowing moments aboard a pitching, rolling slab of steel always reminds a seaman of his own mortality. Those who don't believe it, have their comeuppance after their first gale.

Mark stood facing the wind remembering the day his own life was turned around by Mabel's healing, back in the old neighborhood. It was good to see others reverence the One he believed in so much. He forthwith puffed some of the seabourne zephyr into his lungs and thought, "How good to be alive!"

It wasn't all that long ago, he reckoned, only two years and a little more since he had been hard at work enjoying the company of these excellent sailors, flying the <u>Corsairs</u> on and off the flight

*Attack of the Koto Maru*

deck doing the maneuvers Uncle Sam so graciously paid for and enjoying his daily run on the flight deck. But he was glad to be in Washington nonetheless and secretly did not miss the carrier as much as he was given credit for. It was a good day to enjoy old friendships and remember those past moments jogging on the ship when a sudden fall on the super-sharp surface of the flight deck could erase the skin from one's knee all the way to the patella.

At the same moment of reverie for the former sailor, on another island Paul Stevens smacked one of Ranar Moolong's servants unceremoniously on the side of his head in the locked room. His fist sent cups and dishes flying. "There, you little twerp! Eat it yourself!"

The jailer's keys came quickly from his belt. Paul stepped to the door saying, "Good ole Ranar, overconfident as usual."

Slowly he creaked the door open and discover he was alone in the hallway. Susan's door was next to his elbow. The key slid easily into her lock but turned with difficulty. After hearing the tumblers click, he opened the door with care and stealth to retrieve his nervous compatriot.

But the steno from Cincinnati showed no mercy in bringing herself forward with a sharp but feminine jabbed punch the second he opened the door. It landed him resoundingly on the floor.

"Oh, I'm sorry," she panted in a whisper helping him regain himself.

"Gawd, lady. Why didn't you do that to our fabled host two days ago?"

"I can do it pretty well, but I need the element of surprise."

"You accomplished that!"

Paul chuckled a moment through the sting of her hit then popped his thinking back to the matters at hand. "I sense you had the same idea about getting outta here."

"Yeah, two days of this is enough!"

*Alan De Wolfe*

"Now we have to figure how we're gonna get gone from here," Paul lamented stroking his chin. "We can't execute a plan if we don't have one."

"Oh, it might not be too difficult to dream one up," Susan returned, dangling the keys to the speedboat in his face.

"Heads up thinking, girlie! My congratulations! So that's what the tantrum was about when we came in on the boat."

"Yep! I snatched the keys and the morons didn't have sense enough to search me. They still think they're lost somewhere."

Before another tick of the clock went by, the duo slipped outdoors through a rear ground-level door, along the patio wall and down the steep hillside using a different route than they had used before. Susan wore a pair of pants and a blouse one of the housekeeping women gave her, but Paul still had only his corduroy shorts and sneakers. It had rained briefly during the night making the jungle growth hiss and drip and steam. Everything was slippery and damp.

Paul spoke quietly, "We'd better not stay on the main trails. Let's go to the right here and around by that waterfall."

He led the way down a side trail, which to Susan was mildly frightening alongside the deafening thrash of water speeding in a vertical-down motion. Along the edge of the descending precipice, everything went well until Susan misjudged her step and slid into an unbalanced choreography. Before Paul could step forward to steady her, she twisted pizzle-end upward into the charging waterflow. She got the barest scream out before heading down the slippery-smooth rock sluice, zooming past her shocked companion at a breakneck clip.

"Hel...!"

"Oh no," he yelled in a whisper.

Distracted by Susan's fall Paul then misstepped on, of all things a fallen banana and headed rapidly in the same direction following the descending woman, shooting downward so fast he could only close his startled eyes.

"Yaaaaa...!"

*Attack of the Koto Maru*

In the dizzying swirl of a nightmare made real he spiraled out of control faster and faster down the perpendicular stream, brushing the smooth rock with fleeting touch, wondering if his next sensation would be splashing into a saving pool or dashing his body to pieces on a rock. Anticipation stopped his mind cold while his flesh picked up speed into the stinging spray from another waterfall off to one side. The converging falls widened and pushed him faster until he thought survival might not be an option.

He sensed a cliff's edge, then a fifty-foot free fall away from the steep, slick rockface. Just as he reckoned there might be no end to the drop, his body plunged deeply into a waiting lagoon in a standing position. His foot bottoms felt the smack of surface waters far below his last remembered, and much softer footfall on a rotting banana. The plunge filled his unwilling nostrils with the sharp intrusive bite of water. In the next few seconds, the cool waters began to slow around him and he felt himself rising almost placidly in an effervescent dash of tickling bubbles. When Paul finally broke the surface and sucked air, Susan popped up near his shoulder appearing unhurt. The roaring splash of water seemed less hurtful but he still had to yell.

"Wow! I'm glad we missed"

"Not by much!"

He swung around to her in the clean fresh-water foam of their remote estuary and was happy to see a smile form on her face. Pulling her away from the noisy splash and into calmer water, he waited until their feet touched sand then planted a kiss on her lips not fully knowing why. It cancelled his own bristling stupefaction. He concluding that a fall from such a height is bound to bring out the awe in one's nature.

Away from the roar of the waterfall, they separated from their ethereal kiss with a snap looking at each other blankly then laughing in controlled hysteria.

"Wow is all I can say, too!" she blurted.

"Whew, I'll say! That was slice of life not for the faint hearted!"

*Alan De Wolfe*

The incident introduced a feeling of mortality to their reeling minds and made one thing clear; that the fearful surprises of life might actually cause them to lose each other. The two flying, flailing human cannonballs sobered up and became serious once more, promising each other a more cautious approach to their dilemma. They climbed ashore and assessed the damage to their supercharged bodies. No significant ruin could be found amidst the tingle of their bones and sinews.

"It did one good thing," Susan said. "It got us down the hill fast!"

"Lady, you've never been more correct! And gave us a darned good bath too!" Glorying in the bright sunlight, the drying rays seemed to make it difficult to think about their task just ahead - stealing a boat.

"Now we need a lot of luck. And I hope that speedboat is gassed up."

A covering of darkness would be a welcome advantage, but it was not to be, in the middle of the day. Fortunately, no workers could be seen near the boat they desired to steal and the whole thing began to look possible. "They're probably off looking for those silly keys," Paul smirked glancing through the trees.

The two desperados re-entered the water from the lagoon at a point just before it emptied round the bend into an ocean inlet. They hurried their paddling quietly through an open area from the shoreline to the steel skin of the container freighter Susan had arrived on. The speedboat lay wallowing in the easy tide immediately past the freighter, whose side looked twenty miles long to Susan. It was also sharp with barnacles. Paul's boat bobbed near the speedboat untouched since they brought it in.

"Sure hate to leave my skiff."

"Get me out of this and I'll buy you one!" Susan quipped.

Their first few swimming strokes were influenced alarmingly by churning currents alongside the ship, but they made their way to the dock pilings past it, weaving in and out until they were near enough to purloin the prize beyond.

*Attack of the Koto Maru*

Meanwhile, high atop the escarpment Susan and Paul had just tumbled down, a groggy servant stumbled into the hallway and called for help. Very quickly his overtures drew a response from Ranar himself who had been walking along his path, trying to decide what to do with Paul. "What do you mean they are gone!" he blazed. "Where can they go? Get me a phone!"

Down at the water, Susan watched Paul slink up and over the edge of the speedboat and into her presence. Something she'd held in her hand was missing. "Oh gawd, I don't have the keys!" she puffed. "They must be under the boat, I just had them!" The beachcomber-turned-commando felt his heart sink. Exasperation surfaced in his voice.

"Oh, for God's sake!"

Paul's own boat was very near the speedboat but too far for a giant step. He allowed himself a small desperate sigh then slipped back into the water and paddled quickly to his boat. "Humph, it's good to have <u>some</u> luck," he lamented.

The middle-aged swimmer yanked himself up into his boat somewhat amazed that no one seemed to be around. He wondered if his luck would continue to hold, and for how long. Would the diving mask be where he left it, in one of the side lockers? "Damn, they're locked!"

In the blink of an eye, he located a steel bar used as a cog for the windlass and pried the cover open with a pop. He grabbed the mask and turned round for a last look. "Breaks my heart to leave you, baby. Hope I see you again."

With mask in place, flashlight in hand and a gripping fear in his belly he dove down into the dark abyss about one fathom too far for his unpracticed lungs. The swirling currents influenced by the nearby ship almost disoriented his senses but he kept searching in the murky depth. He made himself touch the sandy bottom often for reference. It was brighter than he'd thought, but the dark sand didn't help.

In the boat, Susan sensed trouble when she heard a phone ring in the small shack across the unloading area. Crouching down, her attentive eyes locked on a dockworker heading toward the receiver. A pit of fear formed in her stomach. She held her breath and tried to read his face.

Exactly under her, far below in the water Paul felt his lungs cry out for air, any air. Even the stagnant air mass he remembered from New York City would have been a glorious relief at this point. But Paul was no stranger to the scuba experience. He kept his confidence knowing his "second wind" would soon kick in. In the gloomy scary muck of water with lungs screaming for relief, his beam of light finally caused the flash of reflection he'd been so desperately seeking. He reached and grabbed the keys to the speedboat.

On the surface Susan saw the worker pick up the phone and quickly look around the dock area. Perhaps Ranar had been tipped off by now. The man shouted some gibberish exciting the other workers nearby. "Uh oh," she said worriedly. They looked in her direction.

Almost instantly, Paul split the calm surface of the water exploding up from below in a shocking splash, gasping in huge breaths for the gaseous mixture his diaphragm always took for granted. "Start the boat now!" he gagged, throwing the keys within.

Susan snatched the keys and did as instructed bringing the languishing racer to life. The sputter-bang of unmuffled pipes ripped a loud signal into the quiet air alerting Ranar's dockworkers and all within earshot. Freddie jumped from his approaching vehicle locking eyes with Susan. It caused her to gear up a little too fast.

The jerky motions of the boat kept an exhausted Paul off-balance whenever he tried to climb in. Without warning the powerful boat snapped both retaining ropes and shot out of the quay more rapidly than either of them expected. It left the partly-overboard man to cling hard to the side rails with a fading steel grip.

"I'm losin' it!"

"Hang on!" Susan yelled.

"I tell you, I'm losin' it! Slow the damn engines!"

*Attack of the Koto Maru*

"I'm trying to figure it out!"

The groper was half in, half out of the water, skipping along with unwilling abandon beside the speeding craft. The furious lashing of salt water intensified momentarily when the boat broke out of its harbor and into the open sea. Paul banged and slammed into the wooden side like a balloon in the wind before Susan finally calmed herself and cut the power. The idling boat slowed so quickly that Paul flipped over and washed forward feet first. The driver let loose of the controls and helped him slither over the edge by pulling on his cold skin. He fumed as much as his panting would allow.

"Good heavens, woman, you could have lost me!" He thunked to the boat's bottom totally out of breath. She answered meekly, "Sorry. I never drove a boat much."

As soon as the gasping cripple could pull himself together, he stood to take control of the speeding machine, happy to notice the seas were calm and placid and visibility was unlimited.

"Oh, what a relief!" he said regaining his breath.

"Look!" Susan yelled from the back pointing at Catena.

Paul shunted around to see two other speedy boats beginning their hot pursuit of the two of them. "Oh hell! Short relief!"

Though the other boats did not seem quite as fast as theirs, it was plain to see that the fugitives from the island "paradise" of Catena might not get away today any better than they did two days ago. The gas gauge stood at half. Paul squeezed his frustration through his teeth. "Aw, nuts! I'm not going back to that friggin' island!"

Above the roar of the engines Susan went to his side and shouted, "Did you hear what they were talking about last night on the patio?"

"No, what?" he returned.

"They're moving their nuclear creations out in four days to their customers, God knows where, in that same ship that brought me here. That would make it Thursday morning early."

## CHAPTER EIGHT

A sharp "putt" was heard behind them just before a bullet ticked the windshield frame in front of Paul.

"Don't hit the girl, you idiot," Freddie shouted at his marksman. "You will be dog food if you do!"

"My God, they're shooting at us," Susan exclaimed.

"Get down, they only want me!"

Because the two were unarmed, the solution dawned on both escapees at the same time. Susan jumped up and said, "I'll stand in front of you! Ranar won't shoot his next wife!"

Paul knew she was right and sure enough, when she stood between him and the bullets the gunfire stopped. But Freddie and crew assumed they needed only to wait for the gas to run out in the speeding boat ahead of them to effect the capture of their slippery house guests. It was like an outing, an easy quest for game and Freddie allowed himself a faint smile. He had plenty of gas, the speedboat did not. "So that's where the keys went."

Paul's mind raced like a needle on a phonograph record waiting for the spike to drop into the right groove. Freddie would have no use for him he was sure and he didn't want Susan to be prey to that self-important potentate from Malua, or wherever it is that feeds his ego so effectively. Paul knew that as long as they were ahead of the bad guys there were always possibilities. "A fertile mind and a little luck," he surmised.

Paul strained his eyes into the wind seeing only one thing ahead of the speeding craft - a craggy rock island with unfriendly landing spots. He'd been on the island before just to explore it. Except for some interesting caves in the high rockface it offered nothing. A small prayer rolled around under his breath requesting some kind of divine deliverance from the whims of Freddie and his misfits. The engines roared mightily, he turned the craft slightly to the left and headed for the rocky port directly ahead. The two would arrive there in minutes. After that they'd be on foot and would have to think of something.

*Attack of the Koto Maru*

On Catena, Ranar Moolong waited at his telescope for the wireless to crackle updated messages from Freddie. Mark Ingram reached Timano about the time Ranar took his next look through the eyepiece.

Anyone who visited Timano was treated to the usual frenzied style of salutation. Mark, the navy man with more than a passing rembrance of these island cultures was being welcomed with much ado. Though he had a mission, a few hours of fun sounded good to him and the food promised to be sensational as always. He saw the seductive dangers in the island ambiance spread out before him, just as he was totally oblivious to the high drama a scant few miles from him which would have to play itself out with no audience, save one telescope.

"Welcome to our little island," Naoki said to Mark. "I am Naoki Matsumoto. Come this way to the foods we have prepared for you."

Mark eyes popped upon seeing the food put forward in lavish abundance. "Thank you, Naoki." Mark wondered aloud, "Is this a special day?"

"Yes, you are here!" he said with a grinning laugh. "Are you just going to have a vacation? How long will you be with us? Why don't you stay awhile?"

Immediately disarmed by the simple people of Timano, Mark decided right away that he liked them, beginning with this accommodating young man. He perceived an honesty and trustworthiness he would need for his spying mission once he found trust and mutual respect. He sized him up and said, "Yes, that's my intention. Say, I want to rent a boat tomorrow, is that possible?"

"Yes, of course! You can rent mine! Or maybe, Ningo's!"

The American was very pleased and felt himself relaxing as a second friendly native shook his hand. He knew that the charming nature displayed by his new acquaintances was a positive omen. The islanders took Mark by both hands and led him toward the interior of the village. In his mind he remembered how much the innocent act of holding hands meant to cultures other than those of the west. "No need for silly masculine dogmas here," Mark chuckled.

During their walking discussion, the young islander Naoki summoned an old man to his side and said, "This is my father."

"Pleased to meet you, sir," Mark intoned.

The old man looked deeply into Mark's eyes and said, "I am also pleased."

The penetrating look from the elder gentleman ran up a flag of caution in Mark's mind for reasons he couldn't name. "Your home is very beautiful."

"Yes, you know we have been here since the great war."

"I understand, sir. I know something of your island, but not very much."

Few people on the island could read the thoughts of the old man like his son. Down deep, beneath the rock-like features of a wrinkled Japanese face Naoki could feel his father's trust of this new visitor. He knew, and it was good to see, that like the earth itself with striations of permanent sediments, friendships evoke thousands of nuances in their layers of structure. The quick trust between the old man and Mark was born of a reverence that only two servicemen would understand no matter what their ideals. Naoki reckoned that it was a thing seldom experienced by those who have not served their country. No one, not even his son knew that the old man might soon reveal the island's long held secret; that he might finally begin to let go of it. To Naoki, his father's trust of Mark seemed like a good thing.

"Come. let's eat some more."

"Sounds good to me!"

"After you eat and relax, I'll show you around our nice home. Hospitality is first on Timano!" Mark loved it, reveled in it, and decided to enjoy the experience to the hilt. For the moment, his mission's importance almost slipped away from him.

*Attack of the Koto Maru*

Later in the afternoon, after much eating, laughing and good conversations Naoki showed Mark to the cabin he would use for sleeping and relaxing.

"Here you are. Just take your rest."

"Thank you, Naoki."

"I'll call for you later. Don't let anything concern you, you are among friends."

The tired pilot knew instantly how the rope hammock would best serve his needs, proceeding forthwith to suspend his weary bones in luxurious levitation. On the front porch of the small battan-sided cottage, Mark drifted into wondrous early afternoon sleep putting off any thoughts of exploration until the next day. The caretaking nature of the people absorbed every worry he ever had and snuffed them out. His snooze came easily.

But events were not as peaceful seventy-some miles from his hammock. Susan had let her guard down and Freddie's marksman took another shot at Paul. Fortunately the seas did not allow a good aim and the bullet went off into plain air. The boat continued its speedy jaunt. "That jackass couldn't hit a stopped boxcar!" Paul said nervously.

Susan returned to his side. Above the roar he said, "Up ahead! That uninhabited island has only one place to pull in. We'll be there in about two minutes. Get ready to run to the rockface on the left at the beach. It has a lot of caves, from its bottom to its three hundred foot top. Maybe we can find a cave somewhere up on those ridges and confuse them. There's a nice easy trail amongst the rocks right where you see that sand hill. It goes up quite fast. Okay?"

"Okay, I'm ready."

With Freddie and friends fast closing the gap between them, they raced toward the only harbor the giant protuberance of limestone had to offer. The rocky island thrown high toward the sky eons ago by some catastrophic movement of the earth awaited their arrival. They had no way of knowing that in a mere ten seconds another surprise would occur. An event nobody including them wanted to see today.

*Alan De Wolfe*

The moment their craft reached four hundred feet from shore, a geological happening became imminent, a happening of great magnitude forecast just two days ago by the jarring earth when they were captured. Paul should have suspected that a small earthquake is often a precursor to a bigger one, the second often monstrous and unforgiving.

Directly behind Freddie's present position and without warning, a booming sound from the deep cold waters of the calm Pacific resounded up through his two boats. It resembled bass from the mega-speakers in the car of a heavy metal maniac passing between city buildings. The water sprang into mad vibration, swirling in every direction, angrily bubbling and frothing its briney foam in frightening syncopation. Some of the rocks on the island suddenly moved in a vibrating blur and one cliff high on the rim off to their right tumbled into the sea. Paul attempted to keep the boat afloat by turning often on a zig-zag course coming in to land.

"My God, what is it!" Susan bellowed.

"Undersea earthquake!" Paul shot back. "Very close! Under us!"

"I've never seen water do that!" she screamed.

Freddie's boat was bobbing almost out of control, thrashing deeply in the foaming swirls, pitching and yawing and vibrating at the quake's hellish prerogative yet somehow staying afloat. He'd brought too many malefactors with him in his two boats and would now experience the regret of it.

All souls aboard the boats hung on for dear life. The mixing caldron of devilish movement made the sea chop with thumping waves in all directions like a magnified version of a crowded swimming pool. Susan held on screamingly, Paul searched his mind for quick answers. Droplets of water lofted in the air and splashed them wet.

After a few seconds which felt like hours, the boat he and Susan were clinging to began to make some headway into the welcome harbor. But it was short-lived. A sudden, frightful motion began to happen. "Oh God, no!" Paul yelled.

"What's happening!"

"Look at the water! It's receding from the harbor!"

"Oh, no!"

"We've got big trouble, girlie!"

His mental hysterics resulted from what he saw in front of them, for the waters of this small harbor were beginning to wash back from shore in preamble to an event few souls have lived through in all history. The woman looked into his face for any tangible shred of optimism. All she saw was apocalypse.

"Get ready for your first tsunami!" he barked to her.

"I hope it's not my last!"

"Be ready to do as I say! You might want to start with prayer!"

"I'm with you!"

"It's gonna get awfully unfriendly around here, but I think the boat's gonna help us!"

If there was anything fortuitous at that moment, it was the fact that they were nearly at shore and coming in fast when the seismic event began. Paul moved his throttles all the way forward to the point of engine overload and started making fair headway despite the receding phenomenon. It was a fast boat with powerful engines and Paul knew this was the last day of its earthly existence.

The firmament had stopped moving hundreds of fathoms beneath them and the water boiled much less, but the new danger was the most fatal of all. Paul didn't know how much Freddie knew about tsunamis but he gave Susan and himself a greater equation for survival simply because of his knowledge. It all hung on one thing.

"I'm gonna run the boat as far toward shore as it will go so brace yourself. It might break all to pieces." Susan put a seat belt on and made one ready for him. "If we don't make it, it was nice knowing you!"

"It's that serious?"

"Yes it is, girlie!"

As fast as it would go, the boat raced flat-out coming into the receding harbor in a blurred straight line.  In a time which seemed too brief, the banging, slamming craft finally ran out of water skidding deftly forward onto the silty sand with a God-awful vengeance.  The disintegrating boat seared their ears with a hissing grind unlike anything either of them had heard before running ahead for many more feet than Paul had dared hope, rocking and rolling and crunching past close boulders which were never more menacing to shipping than this very second.  The two frightened passengers rode the highballing express straight ahead expecting death at any moment from splintering wood or a quick rollover.

But it didn't happen.

The valiant craft served them well dashing forward over sand pebbles, bewildered fish and some very convienent gooey seagrass.  The grass provided a slick surface which actually picked up their speed noticeably before the beleagured hull finally ground to a halt on dry beach sand.  When the spent conveyance stopped oddly intact, the two inside removed their hands from their eyes, looked at each other blankly and unsnapped the belts.

"Lets go!  Head for that sand trail!"

"Oh, my God!  It's <u>vertical</u>!"

"Be glad of it!"

"I'm way ahead of you!" cried a fleet-footed Susan.

Paul was having trouble believing the luck of their astounding boat ride even as he bumped Susan ahead faster.  A misplaced feeling of accomplishment bubbled inside him.  They quickly reached the base of the rockface and turned to negotiate the upward trail.

Several hundred feet behind Freddie, the third boat had capsized, with its seamen swimming about in shocked confusion.  Freddie and his crew tried to make headway in the fast-receding water but the powerful motors were ominously inadequate.  It didn't bode well that he was much farther back in the draining wash than Paul and Susan had been.

*Attack of the Koto Maru*

The backward motion did nothing but increase. Large fish were left flipping everywhere on the damp valley of the harbor, several old hulks of boats sunk in years gone by were again exposed to the sun they'd once known. Ghosts seemed to fly from them.

Racing and panting in their climb up the rockface, the two escapees paused to look back at a sight seen by few living humans; the emptying of a harbor's waters and the impending doom it spelled for the pitiful humans riding upon its regression. Farther out to sea a darkish line appeared and stretched from horizon to horizon, left to right. It was the top of a wave of awesome proportion whose bottom was on the sea floor and whose power was the stuff of legend. Thus came the dreaded tsunami.

"Keep moving, we have about two minutes to get as high as we can!"

Paul had just said the words when a loosened rock hit him on the head. It caused him to nearly lose consciousness and slump to the sand.

Susan backed down the hill, grabbed his arm and shorts and to her own astonishment yanked him to his feet. In a groggy state he still had his wits about him, enough to move his legs as she assisted him, but they were only about sixty feet above the harbor and the dread of a slamming, watery death spread adrenaline quickly through her body. "I don't see any caves," she screeched. "What if we don't make it?"

"They're further up the mount! Move it!"

Upward and upward the woman stumbled with a dazed Paul in tow hoping to avoid the certain destruction Freddie faced. His boat had been resolutely placed on the harbor floor where it remained on the soggy sands of earth not exposed to air anytime in this millennium. He looked behind at his men and screamed, "Get to the shore!" In the muck of very wet sand with large fish flipping all around him, he and his cutthroats struck out for shore a daunting three-quarters of a mile away. The men hurried as best they could in the sucking mire toward the bright beach of their salvation looking into an emptied, V-shaped harbor with an ascending floor. Freddie saw the two runners in flight up the rockface trail and gnashed his teeth bitterly. He had about two minutes to live. Paul looked briefly down at him.

"Nothing except a visit from Christ himself can save them now."

Far up the cliffs on a path surprisingly easy to negotiate, Susan helped her awakening companion to an overlook. They had reached some caves and Susan thought it was high enough. Paul came out of his stupor and abruptly pushed her further still holding his hurting head. A trickle of blood mixed in the sweat of his brow. "Come on. This may not be high enough!"

"Look out!" she shrieked.

Paul jumped out of the way as a teetering boulder lost its balanced fulcrum and pounded past them bouncing its way down the trail breaking off stalagmite protuberances as it passed. "Whew! That was close," she said in a voice singing with nervous tension.

They stopped a moment to regain composure. She propped herself against a stone spire sticking up on the outer side of the cliff and looked radiantly beautiful despite the desperate moment. Breathing heavily they held each other up in a trembling embrace. "Thanks for your help back there," Paul said. His chest heaved, he looked blankly out to sea. "You're a pretty tough..."

His eyes focused back to sea level, wherever it was, in time to see a sight beyond awe, a sight seen before by very few who survived to speak of it. Within his trembling embrace, Susan perceived in his widening eyes a shocking fright not seen yet in their time together. She felt a sweep of emotion race through him and turned to join him with a stare of her own. They gasped in unison.

"Oh..."

Saying nothing more they both looked below and outward at the most incalculable force ever known to exist on this water-wealthy planet. They were dumbstruck to see uncountable trillions of gallons of water rising in heinous proportion into a wave of ascending height. Its rush toward the island began to blast into and over the receded waters of the harbor.

Still out about a half mile, it formed itself into a hideous wall of dark destruction and moved into the empty harbor with unstoppable velocity. It blotted out a major segment of the sky blowing gales of misted clouds off its rising crest. Such was its power that lightning charges could be seen dancing on the breaking wavetops. Freddie and his men looked like ants at a picnic in Hades by the river of lost souls. The disaster came forward with unbridled fury.

In reality the massing wave was slowing, piling itself behind and upon the slower receding water. The wave came in fast at first, then reduced itself in velocity from its top speed of hundreds of miles per hour to fifty or sixty miles per hour. Its reduction in velocity caused it to build predictably to a megawave of indescribable height. Amidst his racing thoughts, Paul knew that despite its speed in the open ocean, the fast wave would be felt only as a mere ripple by ships passing directly over it. They would see only the tip, and then, they would have to be looking for it. It would be imperceptible to them except for a chance sighting.

But when a wave like this is met with the ascending floor of a particular-shaped harbor <u>and</u> the back-rushing waters of the harbor, as was about to happen, it would build from the ocean's floor to unthinkable heights causing the hapless people immediately below it to merely turn and face their fate. Utterly nothing can save a human who is too close, from total annihilation and no structure man has ever conceived of building can withstand it. Paul estimated the height of the present wave to be about a hundred-forty feet and climbing.

High on the sand trail, the two who were relatively safe stood transfixed watching the majesty of the incalculable power of God raise its green wave higher and higher in the bright afternoon sun. On this otherwise beautiful day, Freddie's demise was a forgone conclusion. Susan and Paul watched as he and his men turned helplessly into the towering shadow of doom, having no choice but to accept their fate. The wave became eye-level with the two climbers.

"Quick, into the cave!"

A few more feet up the trail a yawning hole in the wall beckoned them with solid hospitality. Into the grotto they fled and got themselves around a corner to huddle close. Paul wasn't sure that even this venerable rock would be able to survive, but time would tell, and there wasn't very much left of that.

A noise like a hundred freight trains filled the sunny day of a southern Pacific paradise. Everything suddenly went dark for the huddlers. "Cover your ears!" Paul shrieked.

The wave crashed into the island with horrific force shaking the entire rockface but not harming its time-worn existence. The top of the wave slammed through the cave opening as a tubular column of speeding H2O shocked Paul so much he nearly lost his grip on Susan. It blew in through every opening they'd noticed and some they hadn't. Total darkness surrounded them during the eruption of the giant wave but their eyes were clamped tight and wouldn't have noticed anyway.

The assault was short-lived but the din was as loud as anything could be. The pressure of water against the air of the cave made Paul's one uncovered ear pop as if he'd stood in front of a gun muzzle during the unleashing of its power. Susan let out a reactive scream and pressed her palms against the sides of her head. In a mere few seconds the two of them could hardly believe how fast the water was gone. The sun shone in. All seemed normal again albeit wet and dripping.

"Wow!" Susan cried, giddy with nervous titillation.

They looked around at a dripping cave that had been a dusty hole for many years and marveled at the disappearing water. After a short pause they removed themselves from the cave, which was still draining in some inexplicable way, and stepped out into a tangle of wires and wood. Water splashed down from places higher on the island than it's ever been, at least in recorded history, and the sun warmed the rocks once again.

*Attack of the Koto Maru*

"Man! I wonder if the wave actually went completely over the island!"

"Looks like it, doesn't it? And look at this wood. It must be one of the boats, or what's left."

Little waterfalls occurred in places where streams might be inclined to happen after a good rain. Rocks were clean and dark with the wet of salty water. Steam began to mist into a surreal fog when the sun once again baked the rockface. Remaining waters were absorbed or drying quickly. The boat they had survived in actually hit near them on the jagged wall and the motor was below them wedged between some rocks. Water raced in a torrent down the sand trail to the restored waterline on the beach below, then died into the sand as its gallons played out. Above them the corpse of Freddie, ruined almost beyond recognition stared vacantly at them. It shocked the daylights out of Susan.

"Aaiigh!"

"Oh, brother! Like a bug hitting a windshield!"

Paul quickly diverted her eyes and hugged her tenderly. He felt a spark of caring for this sweet girl who didn't deserve this situation nor the wicked attentions of the bad boy from Malua.

But survival seemed to be something they did well. In their minds there was no sense thinking any other way, even though survival might prove to be a continuing problem. As long as they had one another optimism seemed to prevail. They hugged in the sunshine and knew they'd done something historic, something to write about later.

From Catena, with powerful telescopes, Ranar watched the tsunami with awestruck reverence. "It makes one feel insignificant," he confided to a guard nearby who spoke soft prayers into the afternoon air. "Freddie will not be coming home today nor will we be bothered with the two Americans again."

## CHAPTER NINE

The quake was felt on Timano and far beyond. About two hundred miles away the seismographs in the Cook Islands read 5.3 on the open-ended Richter Scale and rumblings were noticed in Australia. Such is the nature of undersea earthquakes. No one with any intellect wants to be near the epicenter. Amongst island peoples, the threat of high waves or full-blown tsunamis is a clear and present danger. On Timano, its deeper harbor provides only a high wave or two, then back to the tranquil place it was only a moment before. The only damage done on Timano was to the nerves of one surprised American as he felt the thud go through the ropes of his hammock.

"What was that!"

Mark got up dazed from the depths of his nap and noticed people hurrying to a cliff outcropping to view something below. Tightening his belt and zipping up, he too rushed to the edge of the precipice in time to see a dark line pass by the island with all speed. It stretched from horizon to horizon causing the waves of the coastline below to churn and foam wildly within the stalwart rocks.

Standing nearby, Naoki said, "Some islands will have a tsunami today!"

Mark had read little about the great seismic sea waves but enough to know he wanted no part of them. This one looked like a tempest in a teapot except for the portentous and fast-moving dark streak. As the island people began to calm themselves he spoke to Naoki.

"Would you show me around a little, Naoki? I love those beautiful cliffs I saw on the way in."

"Yes, let's go along the top of them. This way," he pointed left and into the sun.

In the old cut descending many flights of steps into the depths of the island, Naoki's father, accompanied by the usual shift of cleaners and painters worked here and there at their

*Attack of the Koto Maru*

stations repairing and keeping their prized possession in fine tune. The workers lifted their eyes briefly at the falling sift of dust in the aftermath of the earthquake's thud but it brought no particular concern to their faces. The island had been there a long time and so had its geophysical "cut".

The long staircase was set into the side of the interior rockface and proceeded down level after dizzying level to the brightly-lit bottom platform. The children of the Japanese men thought little about the height of the staircase for they'd run up and down it since they were toddlers.

But few of the women came here because it scared them half to death. It was a place for the men to fiddle with the island's great secret and to admire the facility they finished all by themselves complete with machine shop. The original materials were provided by the old Imperial Navy, but over the years the men had to be more clever, ordering this or that to be brought in by occasional merchant ships. Through it all, deep in the recesses of this volcanic island the secret located in the natural cut of earth was allowed to remain so. Until today.

"Ouch!" Naoki yelled.

"Oh gosh, that's quite a wound," Mark was very concerned after his guide slipped against a rough tree.

Naoki cringed at the sight of his own blood. "Up on that ridge there are some aloe plants. Break off a piece for me will you?"

"You bet!"

Mark climbed about thirty feet to the edge of a large field of boulders which looked oddly unnatural, almost plastic, and without vegetation. He stepped gingerly toward the patch of aloe.

Beyond the patch he saw a huge plant a few feet further which seemed to him a better pick. The long green shanks of vegetation under his stride partially hid a fallen sign written in English. The toppled sign passed by his feet as he advanced further to the large plant. The obscured message read, "Danger, go back!"

*Alan De Wolfe*

Below, Naoki suddenly realized where they were and alarm hit him. "Don't go past the sign!" he shouted up to Mark.

From above he heard, "What..."

A ripping crash was the next sound registering in Naoki's ears when canvas and fiberglass split wide open. "Oh my God!" he screamed, running to the top of the mound.

Approaching the hole where Mark fell in, the terrified islander could hear the end of an echoing yell as his guest plummeted down end over end through the filtered light of the abyss, hitting nothing, touching nothing.

"Yaaaaaa..." Mark exclaimed, falling farther and farther from where he'd been only a second ago. It struck him that he was on his way to hell.

Naoki arrived at the hole and looked down on the old familiar sight. He quickly calculated in his mind that Mark would miss the decking and hit the water. He hoped he could swim.

From below, in the glow of the work area Naoki's father looked up from his polishing in time to see the human cannonball careening down from a tear in the roof. "What's this?" he mouthed. His brow wrinkled above his upward glance.

Spa-LASH! Mark hit the water with a force that made the mighty deck rock slightly in the wash of concentric energy. The workers and the old man rushed to the bow planking and looked over the side at the widening circles awaiting whoever was below the water.

Mark's nose smarted from the pint or so of salty brine roaring fast through his nostrils, but he eventually popped to the surface hacking volumes of the stuff.

After having been in the bright light of day his eyes were slow in adjusting to the indoor lighting as he bobbed within his own concentric rings. It seemed to him he might have plummeted all the way to the great underworld of legend, though he never pictured it this wet.

He touched the metal of a ship's prow still wondering what hit him and looked up the wall of its huge ghostly side. Along

*Attack of the Koto Maru*

the top railing, far above the water each friendly face of the astonished islanders exhibited a puzzled concerned expression. Slightly beneath them the enormous letters of the ship's name overpowered him. It was an outsider's first sighting of a ship known only on this island. The ship's name was <u>Koto Maru</u>.

Naoki made his way around to the entrance, threw open the upper doors and appeared at the very top of the staircase. He yelled down in a panic, "Father, is..."

"He is okay, my son," the old man bellowed back up the metal staircase in hollow echoes. The old man beamed a wide grin. The rest of the workers laughed nervously. "But he is very wet!"

Naoki raced down the steps swiftly while an incredulous Mark Ingram found his way to the dock platform. Naoki came running up still bleeding from his chafed forearm just as the workers helped their guest up the ladder.

"My God, you okay?"

The electrified lieutenant sputtered and caught his breath. "Yes, but I may need fresh underwear!"

Naoki's best friend Ningo chimed in and pointed upward, "See there! You're not a very good guest. You've knocked a hole in our roof." Again the men laughed, each one of them relieved that not only did the American survive, but now <u>he knows</u>. The secret exists no more! He found their battleship! Naoki jumped to his father's side.

"Now, father! This is the time."

"Yes, son, you are correct. It seems we have no choice."

The elder Matsumoto walked over from the ship's deck to the dock platform and realized that after all this time, some fifty years, his son was right. It was the moment <u>indeed</u>. He came closer to the gathering group and began his long utterance to Mark, who had sat on a capstan.

"In the last days of the great war, the Imperial Navy could see the futility of the whole thing. We were losing."

"This ship, 'hull 719' as it was known, was the last ship ever built by the government. The first three ships were named

Yamato and Musashi and Shinano and were considered by the world to be the very best designs ever conceived for battlewagons."

"I know of them, they were the best ever!" Mark said.

"I've read a lot since then about other ships and was always proud to know the rest of the world respected our designs." The old man began unfolding a fascinating tale of eleventh-hour deception regarding the secrecy of this fourth and final ship. It was a complement of sister ships predicted to win the war for Japan.

"The Koto Maru, ah...I named it myself, was not quite finished when, in the middle of the night it was spirited out of the builders finishing yards and taken full speed across many miles of open ocean with only about five hundred of her war-ready men to operate the ship. We did a valiant job of getting our 'little boy' to this island which we held. Normally the ship would have about twenty-five hundred men. We chose this island because of a very large cut in its middle. The cut is located where we presently stand but as you now know, it has been roofed over to hide our ship."

"I don't believe it," Mark said, aghast. "You are the same men...?"

"Yes, we are! Using as much stealth as possible, we completed a zig-zag course and remained undetected until reaching this place. A berth had been prepared for us and we backed the ship into the cut even as the workmen were completing the fiberglass ceiling and doors. As you can see, the doors begin at the waterline and go about six stories into the high place from which you did your circus act." A murmur of mirth hummed through the crowd of men. Mark was beside himself with admiration for a project of this magnitude. "Only the Japanese..." he thought. "You mean this ship has been in this dock for fifty-some years?"

"Yes. We Japanese can keep a secret."

"Yes, but I'm glad the damn thing is out now!" Naoki asserted with his friends' murmuring approval.

*Attack of the Koto Maru*

His father ignored the comment and continued. "The section you fell through may have been weakened by today's earthquake. The big ship has not seen daylight since 1944 and is in a state of perfect preservation. We work on it all the time and the cool of this chamber keeps the ordnance as fresh as the day it was made. We start the engines once a year and keep a fresh supply of fuel ready. We have finished the chamber ourselves and made the outside of the big doors look just like the rocks. Did you not see signs above warning hikers not to go further?"

"No. But I remember thinking the rocks didn't look quite as they should."

"Perhaps some of our paint is fading. But to continue, it takes about four hundred men to staff the ship well enough to do some war action, but the full complement of twenty-five hundred is better of course. All our boys, well, they are men now, have been drilled in every way possible for battle though they have never been out with the ship. Call me a foolish old man, but I thought it was a good thing."

"Yes, and we have loved the drills!"

Ningo's sarcasm caused a snigger of laughter as Mark spoke up, "This is an amazing bit of history here. You should all be proud of this magnificent vessel! I know what happened to the other ships, but tell me anyway."

"Well, in the first place we Japanese tend to use the male gender when thinking of our ships, maybe sometimes female. The other 'boys' were lost in combat. The <u>Musashi</u> was heavily damaged in the battle of the Sibuyan Sea in the Philippines and capsized a few days later. It lived longer than it should have mostly because of the resourcefulness of the men. The ship absorbed nineteen torpedoes and about ten bombs and never sighted an enemy ship. It went down October 24, 1944."

"The <u>Shinano</u> was next. It had been converted hastily into a super carrier just after the battle of Midway and was torpedoed and sunk in November, 1944 by the American sub, <u>Archerfish</u>."

"Then the <u>Yamato</u> was also involved in the greatest sea battle yet in history in the Leyte Gulf of which the battle of the

Sibuyan Sea was a part. The <u>Yamato</u> was recklessly expended in the battle for Okinawa but never got close enough to sight the island. It absorbed intense U.S. Fifth Carrier Fleet strikes in the eastern China Sea and sank April 7, 1945. It had taken ten torpedo hits and about six bombs. So much for superior design." Naoki's father took a breath to keep the sadness out of his voice.

"From March 1945 onward the Imperial Navy pinned its hopes on a last ditch effort by specially trained pilots. Unfortunately the kamikaze attacks were used against the ships best equipped to ward them off, the carriers. Though brutal damage was inflicted, not one ship was lost as a result of these attacks."

"That is an amazing story," Mark said with a reverence in his voice. "I see you've done your homework."

"Yes, and it will be a great story about our hidden ship. Now it will all come out!" Naoki spoke quickly, followed by the thunderous applause of his friends, the other "boys" of these very old commandos. "This is something wonderful to share with the world!"

"My son should show more respect," the old man roared.

He turned and walked off resolutely leaving Naoki the sting of remorse. He loved his father, but knew in his heart that this day had brought the unexpected light of day to their small island nation, much in the same way Mark's gaping hole in the roof showed the first light of day to an old battlewagon after decades of dark secrecy. It was a good secret while it lasted, but to the young islanders it was a relief to have it out at last.

Mark spent the rest of the day looking at the new/old ship with absorbed fascination. On his guided tour Naoki apologized to Mark for his selfish attitude and was promptly reminded to apologize to the one he offended. "My father is privately happy to have the secret known. Don't be fooled by his gloomy look."

"The ship has nine - eighteen-inch guns, twelve - six-inch guns, twelve - five-inch anti-aircraft guns, twenty-four - twenty-five millimeter anti-aircraft guns and four - thirteen millimeter anti-aircraft guns. It has sixteen-inch armor plating on the main

*Attack of the Koto Maru*

belt, seven-inch plating on the deck and twenty to twenty-five-inch plating on the turrets. It displaces sixty-four thousand tons empty and seventy-one thousand tons fully loaded. It is eight hundred sixty-three feet long with a beam of one hundred twenty-seven feet. Finally, it has a draught of thirty-five and a half feet and the maximum speed is supposed to be twenty-seven and a half knots but I think we could get much more. At least we young guys would like to try!"

"You certainly know your stuff, Naoki."

"It's been drilled into me since I was old enough to say da da," the young man said, laughing.

Mark took a moment alone to consider this incredible discovery. He was sure the islanders would have a world-breaking story when at last they tell the media. When Naoki went across the deck under the towering superstructure to instruct Ningo on some small point Mark walked off by himself, his head buzzing with the old man's tale of the Japanese Navy's last days. "Wow! Admiral Ingram will be astounded! Wait until he finds out!"

The ship's deck he was strolling on disappeared into the far shadows of the dimly lit end. Eight hundred sixty-three feet of overall size couldn't be easily contemplated because it filled the cut in the island so completely and didn't allow a long view. The ship disappeared into darkness, front, back and to the tops of the upper structures from whence Mark took his tumble. He could see workmen busy repairing the brilliant hole high above through which he careened. The whole thing was overpowering to think about and in a few minutes, he made the cheerless discovery that the stairs one uses to escape this cavern were indeed dizzying. He wasn't afraid of heights but found himself climbing the steps toward the door with sure-footed caution.

Naoki rejoined Mark as he stepped from the upper doors at the top of the island returning him to the surprising light of a lengthening day. "That was the most moving afternoon of my life, Naoki. Well, that is, except for a certain Christian revelation some years back."

"Yes, it must rank right up there with the best," he said chuckling. "Come, I'll show you the sloop we will be using tomorrow for your tour of the islands. Then I have to go and make a plan to tell this whole thing to the world. My father wants me to handle it."

"If I can help, I'll be glad to."

"Thanks. I might ask."

Mark sank again into contemplation. "A change of command from father to son," he said to himself. "Appropriate."

# CHAPTER TEN

Paul Stevens said a few Christian words over the burial mound of the unfortunate Freddie, the only one whose body was recoverable on this nameless rock island he presently shared with Susan Black. He presumed the other cutthroats were shattered to bits or carried completely over the island. The thought was appalling.

"I'm really sorry for him," Susan said quietly.

Paul replied pragmatically, "Rest assured sweetheart, old Freddie wouldn't have done the same for either of us."

It was the morning after the giant wave and the sand of the beach felt good to their toes. It looked good too, having been reshuffled to a pristine cleanliness in the gigantic sweeping tsunami. Susan and Paul were glad to have survived one of nature's most frightening spectacles. Paul already had it in his mind to write a book about it. After all, a first-hand account by a survivor is a thing the world needs, especially regarding the elusive tsunami that few have seen. The money from such a book might get him another boat.

"We're lucky in some ways, unlucky in others."

"How's that." Susan asked.

"I'm sure Ranar thinks we're as gone as Freddie. But there's no fresh water on this island."

Paul knew his words were true for he had scouted the island once before. Its lack of water is what took him to Catena in the first place. He held Susan's hand and walked up and down the beach with her looking for signs of survivability on an island with no fresh water. There was also no way to prepare foods if they could catch something in the shallow waters. Paul kept his sense of humor.

"So. Ever had raw fish?"

"I will if you will."

Susan laughed and threw her head back. She enjoyed walking with Paul and found a lot to admire about him. Paul was happy to have simply survived, but he was more tuned-in to what their needs would be than his companion. They walked side by side and enjoyed the balm of their friendship. It was a friendship born of trust and kindness for each other, a friendship free from the stress of Catena Island and the dirty little potentate's son they'd come to dislike. Real freedom from Catena Island was a soothing salve to their small cuts and bruises. However, by early afternoon thirst was creeping up on them.

"It looks like our only way out of this is to try to swim to that green island over there. I've been on it and it has water. Looks like it's about six miles. Gawd, I don't know if we can do it. What do you think, Susan?"

"I don't know what to think. But I know I'm glad to be away from the royal brat, what's-his-name."

Paul mumbled his concurrence and they spent the next hour considering their tenuous chances. He knew there was fresh water on the other island, but such a distance. And who's to say what great carnivore of the deep abyss might be watching. He wasn't sure, but he thought he'd seen some box jellyfishes wash up on the beach over there. If so, no one with any knowledge or good sense would go near its waters. Those jiggly denizens of the deep are earth's most venomous creatures causing a dreadful death within four minutes. They're thought to be located only near Australia. Maybe he was wrong about it. He hoped so anyway. But what awful anticipation to the swimmer!

Out on the broad ocean and not too far from the tsunami-washed rock island, Mark sat aboard the sloop <u>Naoki I</u> at the stern daydreaming. "Why <u>Koto Maru</u>?" he said to his guides.

Naoki gave the wheel to Ningo and went aft to speak more easily. "Well, my father married a native girl who was very beautiful. But she died shortly after my birth which left him devastated and melancholy. She loved to play a small harp he had managed to get from somewhere and as it has always made him think of her, he named the ship after the harp which is <u>Koto</u> in Japanese."

*Attack of the Koto Maru*

"Where does <u>Maru</u> come from?"

"I think it is a nautical term meaning 'little boy' which Japanese mariners use to speak affectionately about their ships. Is it silly?"

"It's no sillier than calling a ship 'she' or 'her' like we do in the west. Actually, I guess we would be east of you."

"Depends on which way you go! Ha ha!"

During his cheerful repartee with Naoki and Ningo, Mark realized he would have to confide soon in these two helpful guys in order to get as close to Catena as he'd hoped. They revealed their island's big collective secret to him, now it was his turn.

"I hope you will forgive me Naoki and Ningo, but I haven't been entirely truthful with you."

"Oh?" Naoki wondered.

Mark stumbled with his thoughts for a moment. "I have reason to believe there is something out of the ordinary happening on Catena." He searched Naoki's face for some approval.

"Like what?"

"I have high-flight...well, spy pictures of the island and it has a large concrete building on it. I believe it is the workshop of a Ranar..."

"Ranar Moolong of Malua," the islander stated matter-of-factly, startling Mark. "Little happens in these islands we do not know about. For instance, see these peaks of rock we will soon pass?" Naoki pointed, "I know it was the only island hit by a tsunami last afternoon. You may not realize, these islands are my backyard." The two Timanoans summoned to their faces a contrived smirk and smiled at Mark's surprise. "Our ears are everywhere."

At the moment of their grinning smile, the small sloop glided by the craggy rockface island of the two Catena runaways. Paul and Susan were lounging on the sand still in a quandary about what to do next when the small boat suddenly putted past their location. It was soundless amongst the heaving swells and broke into view without warning beyond some rocks. At first neither of them noticed the little boat, being in intense conversation with their sides to the water but after a second, at the edge of her peripheral vision Susan saw the bright flash of someone's white shirt. She jumped to her feet. Paul was nearly as quick but couldn't quite keep her from that first shout of desperation.

"Hel...!"

He cupped his hand over her mouth and hoped the people were friendly, for sure enough, they had heard her and waved an acknowledgement. "Did you stop to think they could be from Catena?" he rasped quietly, holding her still.

"Hello there," Mark called out from quite a distance. His two shipmates brought the boat around and aimed it toward the splashing beach surf.

"Hello," Paul returned tentatively. When the boat closed in he again shouted. "Where do you come from?"

After the vessel crunched into the beach Mark hopped off speaking. "Well, I'm from the States and these guys are from Timano. Where's your boat?"

"Tsunami got it," Susan chimed.

"Oooh."

"You are very lucky to survive such a thing," Naoki returned, sizing up the pretty woman and being immediately attracted. "I can hardly believe you are here!"

"Us, too," Susan added.

When Mark jumped from the boat he also turned his attention to the prettiest of the two. A glint of recognition moved through his mind. "Wait a minute. Have I seen you somewhere?"

Susan shaded her eyes and squinted, "You're one of Admiral Jessup's aides, aren't you? Mark..."

"Yes, I'm Mark Ingram and you're Susan...Black, right?"

"Yes, this is incredible!" The two followed by saying in unison, "Why are you here?"

"Wait a minute! You were the one kidnapped! It fits!"

"That's right. Spent a few days in a damn container. It's a rotten way to travel, I'll tell you!"

Paul jumped in. "But you did it in a Ferrari!"
"Huh?" Mark said, confused.
"I'll explain later."
The gravity of the situation hit Susan and Mark at once, though they did force a small laugh. Amid looks of puzzlement from Paul, Naoki and Ningo, Mark changed his expression from confusion to smug and said, "It appears we have a few things to talk about, my dear."

Out to sea, way beyond their conversation, Admiral Ingram's voice rang through the Nimitz. He barked a few orders to his staff as Lieutenant Scott Sheldon transfered commands to the bridge. The big beautiful landing strip finally got underway. Sheldon read down the list of ships in the area and made the decisions expected of him.

"Lieutenant I want to avoid getting too close to the two merchantmen heading this way. Lay in a course due north twenty miles then correct left. That should take us well above them and into the open sea."

"Aye, sir!" came the textbook reply. The concerned lieutenant reviewed the nuclear carrier's recent problems. "But the gearbox may have to be stopped again, sir."

"Oh, great!" was the response. "Are you kidding?"

"No sir. We'll know in a little while. It would only be for a couple of hours again."

Admiral Ingram could only sigh and continue to talk to himself the rest of the day. For him, the only entertainment onboard was viewing the radar scopes. The green was restful to his eyes.

On the same big ocean not too many miles west of the admiral's position and heading south-southeast, the Balboa lumbered into the radar patterns of the Nimitz. The old ship was in a crossing course with the carrier, though it would be early Tuesday morning when they drew near. Admiral Ingram roared, "And old bushel-butt Jessup is on the Balboa. Give her lots of room or the jackass might hit us!" "Aye, sir!" Sheldon threw back.

At that moment it was late afternoon and the group ashore on the tsunami-washed island-with-no-name had concluded their long, twisting stories. Noaki and Ningo listened to the castaway's tale with curious fascination.

Mark said, "So you see, we've got to go to Catena and let me get a look for myself."

Paul quickly interjected his negative, "No way, man! In the first place I'm not going, period, and in the second place, you can't go anyway. The guy's got security up the ying-yang. Nowhere can you touch that island without being detected."

Susan added, "And I'm not going back to that stinkin' island a third time!"

Naoki looked at Ningo and snickered. "It's not so difficult to land on Catena. And what is 'ying-yang'?"

Paul ignored the question. "Oh? And I suppose you two can find some wonderful place to land?"

"Of course," they chuckled with an airy jaunt. "This is our backyard."

Susan fought the idea and so did Paul, who was still glaring at the two islanders. But what else could they do? Paul knew that if they let the small boat leave them without getting aboard, who's to say it would ever come back? Maybe Ranar's men would discover the boat and put Mark and the two other guys in his prison. Reluctant as they were, there was no choice.

"Couldn't you take us to Timano and come back?" Susan asked hopefully.

Mark said, "Too far. I have faith in these guys. They know their own area very well. It should only take a little while. Lets eat here and sneak over to Catena at dusk. Tomorrow is Tuesday, and if he's shipping his devices on Thursday we'll be able to do something about it." Mark remembered his uncle on the <u>Nimitz</u> might be near enough to make a difference. "I have to be sure."

Later that evening as dim light overtook the beautiful southern Pacific seas, a boatload of people tossed together by life's odd happenstance set out for the nearby island of Catena

*Attack of the Koto Maru*

and their assault on the big unlit bunker. The concrete structure had a backside Paul had not noticed before, which, being set within the covering brush, rose darkly above the tree line. The bunker wall over on the side chosen by Ningo and Naoki was big, dark and scary. Stealthily, their boat came within sight of the projected landing spot moving beachward over liquid mounds of moonlit foam. Susan and Paul were back again to their most hated paradise.

Ningo said, "See? For some reason this side is not guarded by the cameras. The guy is very arrogant."

"We already know that."

"To him, security on the backside is not needed because the wall is so high. Also, no guards are here because they think no one can land here. But we are good with this boat."

"Yes you are."

Paul discovered that it was hard to wipe the smile from the faces of the beaming boatmen. They went about their duties with the whites of their eyes and teeth glistening in the ghostly light of nighttime on the water. Their savvy seamanship impressed him and taught him a few things in the meantime, adding an element of respect. It was fun to help them handle the boat and it made him sick of mind to realize his own boat was no doubt, gone forever. He worked with intense determination to take his mind off such thoughts.

Before long they drew near shore. The polished decks of the Naoki I shone a reflective shine beneath very limited moonlight. Under his breath Paul said to Susan, "Never thought we'd be back here. In fact I never thought we'd be anywhere after that seismic wave." She agreed quietly, "I'll second that."

The boat's super-hushed engines were a boon to them tonight in their mission of island intrigue. Everything was peaceful, as if nothing were amiss except for the squeaking beetles and prolific creature sounds. They rode a low breaker until the boat came in against the sand. Soon they had tied up to a close palm. Paul whispered to Susan. "Welcome to the island you can't seem to get away from." Naoki pointed at the endless wall of concrete.

"Now I will show you how you can get your peek into that big thing."

"Okay," Mark said. "No need for us all to go."

"I had no intention," Susan confided.

"So, how do I do this?"

The last time Susan saw this side of the bunker she was in a speeding Ferrari narrowly missing the wall's edge. At this spot the bunker came right near the roadway and began its frightful rise only a few feet above the swizzling surf.

"Is this how you get up there?" the woman asked, pointing at a step jutting from the concrete.

"That is correct Susan," Naoki said. He observed her with a lingering pause and filled his eyes with her shape. In point of fact, all the men on the Naoki I were quite taken by her. Ningo was the only married man among them but the other three in the party held silent romantic thoughts inside them. Each one was struck with his own private thoughts of appreciation. Her honesty and fresh look had charmed them all despite their trying situation.

Mark looked almost straight up the wall at the U-shaped step rungs attached to its side. The rusty appendages disappeared abruptly into the dark mists of night. "You mean I have to climb this?"

"It's the only way. I have been up it many times and they have never known it. The first section is about sixty feet, then there's a small balcony. I guess the guards use it for their coffee break."

"Then the next section is about seventy-five feet high and you will arrive at a wide ledge, where there is a door. You can try the door, sometimes it's unlocked, or use more outside steps to go up to the very top, another seventy-five feet or so. Shall I go too?"

"No, Naoki. Two might slow us down. I just need a good look at the operation. Then I can finally give Jessup enough evidence to act."

When Mark began his ascent, he looked up at seemingly hundreds of step rungs and wondered how long he would recognize any constructive thoughts in the thick miasma of terror occupying his mind. He was not afraid of heights but this was really high. And on unprotected step rungs. It didn't help a bit to know the walls leaned slightly inward.

The landing party looked skyward with its collective eyes locked on the intrepid lieutenant. He stepped rung after rung to the highest part of the first section and carefully peered over the edge to scan the balcony. His eyes beheld only a few chairs and tables with tin can ash trays full to the brim.

Over the rail he flipped, crouching for a moment low on the balcony to look again. He began his ascent up the second section with the effervescent inkling that this section was high enough for a killing fall should he miss his step. Droplets of sweat combined on his forehead and rolled off the cliff of his nose. The skin of his hands hurt from the scratchy rust of the metal steps as upward he puffed.

The second "plateau" was a wide ledge and rail with a door in the wall as Naoki had said. Upon reaching the ledge, Mark panted and popped over the rail to the less frightening "porch". He leaned himself against the wall to catch his breath and release a reserve supply of courage. At least for the moment, he had a floor under him.

In the humid steam of the high balcony he slowly reached for the door knob. The motion was duplicated in a dead heat between himself and an unknown watchman on the other side. At his very touch, the knob turned and swung out boldly.

Mark's hand snapped back to his side. He stood rigid in the blackness behind the open door. A sentry briefly poked his head out for a quick look. Wishing to be anywhere but here, Mark froze his glance behind the guard's right ear and waited to be discovered. The man could see little due to a great difference between the light inside and the lack of light outside. Fortunate for Mark, the guard satisfied himself with a brief glance forward and slammed the door shut. It was at least fifteen seconds until

*Alan De Wolfe*

Mark could jump-start his heart and rekindle his bravery. He had been numbed breathless. "This is not for me," he breathed. In a moment he resumed his regular heart rhythm and tried the door again.

The knob turned easily with no sound. He opened it a crack. Two guards went quickly past in loud discussion adding another shock to his tingling flesh. After their conversation faded, he opened the door enough to enter inside scuffing his shirt roughly across the door sash. He came into a hallway which had other doors on the opposite wall.

When he opened one of them he heard talking somewhere beyond a bulkhead of steel slats which he assumed held up the superstructure. The cavity afforded cover for his spy mission. In the dark area behind the struts his stride took him to an opening near the voices. The sliding door in the roof was closed.

He approached a slit in the wall just right for viewing. A column of light danced on his face while he came closer and fixed himself to look through its bright ray. A whisper echoed through his mind's recesses when the vivid light of the laboratory splashed a reflection off the bomb casings. "Good God a'mighty!"

Mark had only seen pictures of these things, bombs on wheels looking very much like restaurant dessert carts. If taken into a building, say, the Empire State Building, they would probably be overlooked even if they were right under somebody's nose. "This is bad," he muttered. "Very bad!" The intruder continued his watch, finally getting the shock of his life; something he never expected to hear, something nearly beyond his comprehension. The shock of it registered quickly, but the implications took their time.

For the other four waiting below, the span of elapsed-time since their new friend ascended the concrete facing was nearly intolerable. "What if he's been discovered," Susan queried.

"I think he's okay," Naoki reassured. "He is a clever guy. Besides, if he had been found, everyone on the island would be looking for us right now."

*Attack of the Koto Maru*

"Look there!" Ningo whispered, pointing into the darkness.

Sure enough it was Mark, gingerly making his way back to them scratching bits of rust from the metal steps and generously speckling their faces with it. His scuffing feet chafed the leather of his shoe bottom.

Jumping from the last rung he leaned on the wall and panted for a moment, gasping, "You were right, there must be eight or ten of those things. They must not be allowed to reach their destinations!"

"Are they still planning to ship them on Thursday?" Susan inquired.

"Yes," Mark puffed, still breathing hard. "I heard them say it. And get this! Admiral Jessup's in on it!"

# CHAPTER ELEVEN

Not wishing to stay on the island of Catena for the night or on the rock island nearby, the voyagers opted to go one island beyond the rockpile and camp on Morena. Unfortunately, the people of Morena, while joyfully hospitable, liked their privacy and kept no wireless for the travelers to use. Alerting Timano would have to wait. The curve of the earth may have prevented it anyway and why crackle the airways with something Ranar might hear with his many crafty listening devices? They would be in for the night except for gala activities celebrating their visit. Food and friendship came from every direction.

Morena, like the other islands nearby didn't get many visitors. The inhabitants knew little of westernization and cared even less. Typical of Pacific islands, a green overhanging canopy of palms provided shade for fishing boat repairs and impromptu confabs of fishing-related talk, while any serious island business was discussed over roaring nightly fires. At the evening meetings, the men shared their problems ranging from lost boats and torn nets to maintaining the reserve pools of fresh water, and the women talked endlessly about weddings, food, men and grooming. Waterfalls abounded on this island of plenty and were offered to the unexpected visitors as shower stalls. Susan waited for no one and plunged in.

"Oooh, I can't believe how warm it is!"

"Move over, girlie," Paul said, following her lead in a splash.

Before long, everyone was under the roar of soothing fresh water happily rinsing the salty discomfort from their skin. Tiny girls shuffled along the water's edge offering herbs and flowers to rinse through the hair to purify and sweeten one's hair and body aromas. Amid their giggles it would have been easy to forget a certain Pacific bad boy whose time on earth seemed appropriate only for the gathering of money and power. Everyone presently in Morena's swizzling lagoon enjoyed their bath to the hilt but kept their priorities straight.

*Attack of the Koto Maru*

Their plan was simple. "We still have plenty of time after we get to Timano to get Admiral Ingram on the radio. We'll get back Wednesday afternoon, right Naoki?"

Naoki chewed on an overripe piece of orange mango and answered Mark. "Yes, easily." He ducked his head beneath the surface as Susan piped in.

"This is the best time to stop the cargo because it's all in one place. If we let it get away, who knows how many directions it may go."

Paul agreed, dashing water from his eyes. "If anything can intimidate them it's that bloody aircraft carrier. Thank God it just happened to be in the area."

But if the gallant crew and passengers of the Naoki I were onboard the Nimitz at the moment Paul spoke, they might not have been so sure. The main gearbox went down again just as the vessel turned to port and headed for the open sea.

"I don't believe it!" Admiral Ingram roared. "Commander, I've got to be in Japan in two days for the arms conference!"

"You may go in a chopper, sir," Captain Owens stated.

The captain, a stickler himself for precision was becoming tired of putting up with the admiral's rantings. He and his lieutenant wished he'd just go to his cabin and stay there. But with such an important figurehead dignifying the ship, neither Owens or Lieutenant Sheldon would give it any more thought. Such is the life of a ship's commander and all who serve under his guiding hand. Always prey to the sitting admiral. Owens talked to Sheldon, Sheldon talked to the crew and everyone got on with the fixing. "Is it my fault?" Owens quizzed under his breath. "It's gonna be a long night."

Owens and Sheldon had island celebrations far, far from their minds as they went about repairing the big carrier. On Morena, night time fires lined the village coastline and Naoki and company ate until well past full. During conversations spoken through masculine burps and grunts Naoki said, "I will alert the people here to keep a watch for the movement of the big ship from Catena. Just in case."

"I thought you said there was no wireless here," Paul said.

"Well, some of the young men here have radio on their boats and if need be, they can go out to sea and hook up with other islands. But it takes a while. Their older people are the same as on our island, they don't want too much progress."

"I know. I hate that," Ningo inserted. The two of them laughed as Naoki said, "Sometimes we get together with other islanders and discuss our old fogies. And we do not mean any disrespect in our humor."

"We wouldn't dare!" Ningo added.

Laughter chirped on as evening hours lenghtened into night. Later, just before thoughts of turning in for the night Paul again noticed Susan's agreeable shape. He walked a short distance down the beach with her, appreciating her and women in general. "Well it looks like we're relatively safe now. Are you going back to your life in Washington when this is over?"

"Not sure," she clipped, slurping a warm drink. "I just want it all to end well. Those bombs worry me, and we are the only ones who can sound the alarm!"

"We'll do it okay, sweetheart. We're nearly home free. The best part is, we're still among the living. Coulda been a whole lot different."

"You said it!"

Paul tried to avoid thinking more of her than he should. In his heart he knew age was against him and besides he wanted to continue being a beach bum if another boat could be found. He decided without fuss to content himself with a very nice friendship and just stay within touch. The girl was a difficult study. He remained somewhat mystified, as he always was about women, but liked her very much.

Mark and Naoki fancied her too. The lieutenant wanted her to go back to the Washington lifestyle she'd found agreeable and hoped they might date. "Who knows," he thought, noticing the walking twosome.

Though Naoki would never say it nor indicate it in any way, he rode high on his passions somewhat aflame for this sensitive

*Attack of the Koto Maru*

western woman. He was convinced that if given the right moment, she would see him as a real prize and Timano would be a place they both visited once a year - maybe. He longed for the disco bars and fast living he knew the states could provide plus he liked dreaming about the educational opportunities. He asked himself, "Do I only fantasize, or will it happen someday?" The island's big secret, the heretofore invisible ship mothballed in a ready state for nearly fifty years, had slipped his mind completely. When Susan was in the picture, anything would!

The men sitting around the small campfire that evening represented a mother-lode in the mining camp of masculinity and good-looks. They in turn noticed the pretty Morena island women but were careful to mind their manners.

Susan sat near the men engaging each in happy conversation. Happy that is, to be off Catena once again and in the near safety of Morena, but she was not unaware of their feelings. Something about a woman just senses those things. It was rather fun to be with guys who each would like to know her better. She scanned their faces now flickering orange with the dying embers of bonfire and counted herself lucky to have met them all. "Each one a man of good character," she thought. "How would a woman chose? And those island guys! Wow!"

Paul, she reckoned, had the peculiar charm of an older, settled man who looked like he was going to live forever. Those gray temples and speckled hair framed his bronzed face much the same way an old hotel in steamy Manila is framed with its encompassing palms. Life with him would be a tender wrap of kindness all the time. What a good guy to come to her aid!

Mark was familiar to her from a party she once attended. His dress blues had certainly set off his tall shape. Throughout that social evening, she'd noticed him several times. From Washington to California, she'd seldom seen a nicer looking guy.

To her, it was equally pleasing to be noticed by the two Timano islanders. But Ningo seemed to be happily married and Naoki didn't seem to notice her much. The unmarried islander had a golden body and flawless physique. His gentle but severe eyes were indicators of strong character set flatly into a doll-like complexion. "The women of Timano must have a difficult time deciding on a beau if they all look as good as these two," she thought.

On a sketch book in her mind she tried to draw the cool and distant Naoki, vacantly applying paint to canvas, rounding his brown torso into his neck and face with her palette knife of wonder. Mark spoke abruptly and knocked her out of her frame of thought.

"We'd better hit the hammocks. Daybreak will come soon enough."

"I'm ready to collapse," Paul said.

His words jarred everyone into realizing how weary they were. All of them dragged heavily toward the hanging tangle of hammocks under a lean-to roof with the islanders arranging stand-up partitions between. Susan could not believe how comfortable the drooping weave was and the perfect night air made her wonder if Washington was really the place to be - ever.

Sleep is bliss, especially after salt-air journeys. Each of the mariners slept the night through in rapt delight enjoying the tropical climate and mysterious lack of flying insects. Just another paradise in the richly blessed Pacific Ocean. Just another island where stress has no presence, and good moments go by too fast. Life here was good.

Morning broke on a balmy Wednesday with increasing air movement greeting them at land's edge. The travelers were soon aboard <u>Naoki I</u> fresh from their dreamless sleep enjoying the splashing surf and watching their sail begin to fill. The quiet engine under them augmented the warm breeze. Another sterling moment on a bright shallow inlet came to life.

Always present, the swelling waves cause one to realize that to be on a vessel on the high seas is to expose oneself to the possibility of getting sick or dying. They are sometimes analogous, but not necessarily. The malaise of seasickness strikes a happier equation than going down with the ship, any ship, but placing one above the other in importance is reserved for those who have done neither.

Two hours out of port were enough to make the prettiest member of the crew sicker than she had ever been in her life owing mostly to the fact that the seas were up, then down, then up again throughout the seemingly endless journey to Timano. Their trip would end in another forty miles, but Susan could take no comfort.

"Oh Lord! I wanna die!" she said from the middle railing of the pitching boat. Paul could not resist exacerbating her problem. "Would you like some mango, girlie?" he chuckled.

"How would you like another knuckle sandwich!" she gurgled, foregoing proper etiquette. He remembered the right jab she splattered him with back in the Ranar's makeshift prison and decided to be a comfort to her instead. He smiled and put his arm around her while she heaved the good food of Morena Island widely from the starboard beam. Mark empathized and wondered why humans try to make jest out of desperation. The poor girl's face was sporting varying nuances of green surprising Naoki and Ningo. They had never seen anyone get seasick. It was nonexistent among their people.

Mark said a few words to Paul. "Susan works in another arm of the Pentagon so she doesn't know Rear Admiral Jessup very well. I can tell you I've never trusted the man. Apparently he and some other brass arranged for Ranar to get some of the more difficult ingredients for his bombs. Bet they're being paid well! Sure blows me away."

"The rat! Where do you think they're going with the devices."

"Who knows. North Korea, Libya, Iran, Syria, they're all potential buyers. Thank goodness we discovered them. I can't imagine what's on Jessup's mind. He was nearly ready to retire with full pension. And those other guys. Weird."

Naoki butt in with naivete. "Western greed, perhaps. I've read about it."

"It real, believe me!"

*Alan De Wolfe*

Paul philosophized, "Ranar must have made a titillating offer. I can tell you from my experience in the business world, money drives people to do some awful things."

Mark added, "Evidently it does in the Pentagon, too. When I went up that ladder into Ranar's concrete box I overheard them say Jessup would be on the island in a day or two. Y'know, I wondered why he gave in so quickly when I requested a vacation. Good thing I didn't tell him where the vacation was to be."

Paul interjected, "Yeah. He'd really be surprised to see your face."

"Wonder how he's getting here?"

Paul inserted, "Prob'ly chopper."

Miles behind their bobbing boat and a few hours off the coast of Catena, Captain Tom Conlin walked the decks of the Balboa thanking his men as he passed them. "Thanks for doing an outstanding job keeping the old girl going," he said walking, shaking a hand here and there. It was still iffy as to whether or not the ship could make Melbourne as planned without some major breakdown, but here they were, doing okay and nearing Jessup's stop. At the stroke of noon on this bright Wednesday the captain was happy to have had good weather all the way, even though the water was a bit choppy at present. "Hmmm. Good day for seasickness," he smirked. No foul weather was expected for the next few days, time enough to get all hands aboard BALBOA to Australia.

"Nimitz off the starboard bow, sir!"

Captain Conlin strode through the outside bulkhead hatch and observed the big carrier from the rail. She was nearly out of sight and stopped dead in the water. He said impishly, "We all break down once in a while, heh, heh." It amused him to think of a monster as big as the Nimitz having trouble. And here he was, on one of the oldest tubs in the Navy cooking along smartly at fifteen knots. "Ensign, send my regards to Admiral Ingram and see if he needs anything."

*Attack of the Koto Maru*

The ensign smiled and dutifully headed for the radio shack to relay the sarcastic message. He passed by Admiral Jessup who was gazing toward the horizon.

"I guess she's laid up for a while," Conlin said alluding to the carrier on the rim.

Jessup replied, "Happens to the best of us."

"I guess you'll be leaving us soon, sir."

"Yes. Thanks for a smooth trip."

"You're welcome, sir."

Jessup tried not to show the delight he was thinking regarding the <u>Nimitz</u>. To him, it was especially good to see the big flattop dead in the water and likewise, Admiral Ingram. The ship would be too far away to be a factor. Relieved and happier than ever, he watched the horizon for awhile then went below and convened his "friends" to a meeting in his quarters.

"How does it look," one of them asked.

"Everything's fine, gentlemen. Don't be concerned about the <u>Nimitz</u>. We're having great luck. She's laid up for who knows how long. I'm glad of it, but we have a good sound plan anyway. Just look after our prized possessions and leave it to me. When we get to the island in a few hours we'll unload the supply box and get off this tub. Then, my friends, Captain Tom Conlin will get the surprise of his shortened life!"

Jessup seemed to go out of his way to prove what a scoundrel he was. His boldness increased with every passing mile. He and his men were having one of their heartiest laughs when Naoki and Ningo were about to dock their little boat at Timano. Ningo threw a line to one of his friends who promptly flipped it around a capstan and slowed their motion into rubber pylons. Susan was helped off the boat feeling marginally better but still aghast at the depth of true seasickness. Naoki said kindly, "Come. I'll take you to a small cabin at the end of the dock. You can rest there, and the green bushes around the cabin will go well with your color." Susan had quite enough of the male humor aboard the boat but managed to say a sarcastic, "Har Har!"

As sapped as she was, it felt good to be within Naoki's strong embrace. He gently laid her in a hammock in a small thatched hut and said, "Rest here. You'll be surprised how soon you'll feel better. Some of the women are here to look after you." Naoki embraced her as she was laying in the hammock. His concern felt unbelievably good to Susan who gloried in his lavish hug. Though stimulated, he retreated to the door.

"You can make the climb to the village when you're ready."

Susan relished the warmth of his tanned, dewy skin and knew she was on the way to recovery. His body aromas were wonderful and she wondered how he did it. Hadn't he been out there sweating with the rest of them? That shower on Morena was quite some time ago. Naoki kept his hot flash to himself and walked back to his boat. He hardly heard the conversations.

"Let's get on the wire to Admiral Ingram," Mark said, helping Paul unload.

Paul agreed but watched further ahead as one of Naoki's friends stopped him on his way back to the boat. The man was animated with words and gesticulations. It punched a few alarm bells in Paul's mind. Naoki's expression changed from humor to grave concern upon hearing the message. He walked back to his fellow mariners and relayed the word. "Our wireless is down!"

"Oh for heaven's sake! Are you kidding?" Paul cried.

"No, it fell over during one of the aftershocks and is severely damaged."

They all looked at each other without speaking being fairly convinced it was an evil portent. They hadn't allowed for this in their thinking. Mark said, "Come on, let's get up to the village and find a solution."

The hike was a thoughtful one for all concerned. On the way up the laborious escarpment, word of their discovery was spreading around the population like a supermarket tabloid headline. Before long everyone was trying to think of an answer to the dilemma, even Susan, who had been brought back to life by one of the island's herbal medicines and was being helped up

*Attack of the Koto Maru*

the hill. She looked at her medicine bottle and said, "What is this stuff? It tastes good and works great!"

One of the women attending her giggled in reply. "It is juice from beetle."

"Oh puke!" she screamed with a rich audibility, muffled only by the rich jungle growth around them.

While Susan made her way up the long trail to the plateau drinking a welcome chaser of water, the men were meeting in a community building. Paul intoned, "Well isn't there any other wireless around? What about the other islands?"

Naoki chimed in, "The nearest radio is about thirty-five miles. I'm afraid it would be very difficult to reach it in time. We can fix ours soon but maybe not in time. If no one intercepts the freighter with the bombs, they could be anywhere in the Pacific pretty quick."

Everyone in the room quickly agreed and turned the place into a loud hullabaloo. Each talked at once and tried to impart his own wisdom regarding the emergency at hand. Mark wanted to take a fast boat, Naoki said there wasn't one available, Paul wanted to get to one of the other islands quick to find a wireless and Naoki's father stood in thought like a man confused. Ningo wanted to wait for the freighter which delivers goods to the island, due tomorrow, and everyone else loudly tried to add their two cents.

In a moment, a knocking sound was heard on the table as Naoki's father began hitting the table more and more forcefully with his shoe. Everyone deferred to him when he finally stood and yelled. The room quickly found its way quiet. His expression changed from the bewilderment it had been at first to one of steely resolve. Everyone focused on his face. No one expected his next words.

"We take Koto Maru!"

# CHAPTER TWELVE

While everyone scrambled for the cut in the island Naoki stood on his small porch, dazed. He'd been sent home by his father to get his Japanese sailors uniform, a request he never thought he'd hear. Every young man had his own uniform and each considered it silly. But it was part of being a citizen of this odd little rock with the big deep slice in it, and he was resigned. After all this time, his entire life, the ship was going out with all its little trained monkeys to show a presence for the good of man. Naoki didn't think he'd be as nervous as this. But he sure was.

The old man was meticulous over the years to keep everything regarding the ship in perfect working order, including the young men who might one day sail it. Anyone with knowledge about the big ship thought the old man overdid it a bit, but no one on the island had much to occupy their time anyway so it seemed okay. It was a matter of pride for the older ones which rubbed off to some extent on the young. Those familiar with Japanese mindset at the time of the war would not be surprised to see the thoroughness of their training transcend itself to this very day. Secrets were kept and duties were done keeping the condition of readiness very sharp in the minds of all. What the elders wanted, they got.

"Naoki!" Ningo paused and reiterated. "Naoki, come! Let's go!"

Still dazed and glassy-eyed, Naoki looked off his porch at his best friend. For once in his life he had no certain words. "I'm coming. I just never thought..."

"Neither did I! But come on! We're gonna make history for the next few days!"

The whole thing was brand-new to Susan and Paul - they'd heard nothing about a secret ship hidden away for decades on this volcanic island. No one had thought to mention it to them. Paul postulated that resting where it is, chances are it couldn't

*Attack of the Koto Maru*

even be found using satellite tracking. It had been tucked away under a shield of crude plastic twenty years before man began using space for the purpose of snooping. Todays telemetry would probably be confused anyway by the steel ribbing in the giant skylight doors, extending from the bottom where the surf bubbled under them to the dizzying heights above. "How could anyone hide a ship that long?" Paul asked himself blankly.

"Wait till you see it," Mark smiled. "The thing is incredible. I found it by accident, and I found it very, very rapidly!"

Susan and Paul puzzled over his words as the lieutenant herded them toward the big door which led down the precipitous staircase inside the cut. They stepped inside on the landing in darkness just as someone below turned on all remaining lights. Owing to the great height Susan let out a scream and jumped behind Paul, who himself reeled momentarily. Even Mark stepped back a bit though he'd already seen it. "Why do women always get behind us," Paul asked, poking Susan with sarcastic fun.

"It's all you guys are good for," she retorted with a slap to his shoulder.

With all the lights on, the big ship below them was of mind-boggling proportion and looked completely new, which it was...sort of. It filled their vision from far left to far right. From the tips of the whip antennae on the highest tower down to the waterline this monster was ready to sail, kept that way day after day, year upon hoary year in anticipation of a time when it might fill the bill for Japan.

Such a need had long been unnecessary in the land of the rising sun, but no one could deny, if the present crew were going to stop the shipment of Ranar's atomic devices, this might be the best way after all. Later they would try to get Admiral Ingram on the radio but now the imperative was theirs alone. It was their destiny to seize the moment, and at twelve midnight or thereabouts, they would sail for Catena to expose one arrogant little would-be dictator to the world. At twelve on the clock they would know what they were made of.

"It won't take long for satellite tracking to notice a giant like this. It will work in our favor, but it's gonna turn a lot of heads!" Mark continued, "No one, but no one is gonna believe this!"

Still cowering on the high stair structure, Susan and Paul got up the nerve to follow Mark down the long stairs toward the old men polishing and oiling the spiffy gray <u>Koto Maru</u>. The old timers already had their uniforms and were looking them over. Mark looked at them and said quietly, "They look like a congressional finance committee wondering if they should spend money on a new ship." Paul and Susan displayed wry smiles.

When the three friends descending on the staircase reached halfway, the door at the top swung open with a crash spilling hoards of young men, some in uniform, some not, down the vibrating stairs like neighborhood kids anticipating the ice cream truck. The thundering group reached the three Americans after they'd hurried to the bottom and jumped clear. The steps shook so much the dock vibrated under their new and shining jackboots.

The men hurried over the gangplanks in long processions, each one eager to reach his assigned station. The sight of the strong deck stretching eight hundred sixty-three feet into the distance and the bustle of preparations of all kinds excited Mark. Paul was contemplative. Susan swallowed hard.

For the next fifteen minutes the young men came in waves. Even the women finally braved the staircase to be a part of the auspicious moment and to see what they might do to contribute to this exciting time. The sudden sea of uniforms and sloe-eyed men sent a shiver through Mark. He uttered an aside to Paul.

"I feel like I'm looking out of a time capsule! Where else could we ever see a muster like this!"

Paul could only say, "Astounding!"

The old men, the original pride of "hull 719" ended their polishing and went below to change clothes. This was the event they'd been waiting for after going about their caretaking duties for years as if war might happen any minute. In truth, it could never have been actual war.

*Attack of the Koto Maru*

One thing the older men were abuzz about was the opening of the giant doors. It was their only serious concern as they looked up from the charting tables temporarily positioned on deck. Each man was not sure the hydraulics would work after all this time. It is the one thing they did not practice weekly. Some of the young men were up on top of the plastic skin knocking away key pieces of the stuff to facilitate the impending grand opening of the huge doors and tidbits fell into the mirror-flat water. Naoki's father was in full uniform on the bridge, the others were in varying stages of proper attire. The old gentleman looked splendid and regal. Naoki opened the bridge hatch.

"Father?"

The old man had tears in his eyes but said, "I'm okay, my son. It is a day, or I should say night, filled with pride for me. We waited a long time to show this, the last of all possible Japanese battleships to the world. I hope it is a world with understanding. I hope the ship will be cared for."

"You will see. It is all okay, father."

Naoki felt a heavy concern for his father, a man of great will and honor and respect. He had never felt such a moment of love for him. "Everything's going to be fine,...sir." Not wishing to lose himself in sentiment the gnarled old man with the weather-worn face turned round on his heel and saluted smartly. Naoki snapped-to as the elder shouted an order.

"Your station will be here on the bridge with me and the original staff. We are old men and will give our direction from here. Your three friends must be kept safe so have them come up here as we sail!"

"Yes, Sir!" Naoki asserted loudly, turning to leave his father's presence. He was beginning to feel some of the same pride his venerated father had kept alive for so many years. When he passed a polished surface reflecting his own military good-looks he suddenly found the fit of the uniform to be rather agreeable. His stalwart reflection with the brass buttons and shiny emblems gave him pause, conjuring up all the ghosts of his father's old bedtime stories, all the former glories of a Japan doomed to fail. He suddenly felt pride in the past - his past. This day of former remembrances would be a stepping stone to the future.

He stiffened and couldn't resist a little smile. "This will be a day to remember!" An old movie cliche found its way to his lips, "Look out, world, here we come!"

The dock area and main deck were swarming with efficient sailors - young sailors drilled week after week to handle their prearranged duties under the close supervision of the old mariners, most of whom could still fit into their uniforms. A couple of the old outfits had been "let out" by understanding wives over the years. Here and there a new patch of material could be noticed. But the snap in their walk and the crack of their commands were as if no time had gone by whatsoever. The young men were confident they could carry on where the elders left off as long as the old ones were onboard to guide them. They had never been out to sea with the Koto Maru. This was the father/son boy scout field trip to end all field trips. To a man, they believed that their fierce group would easily have the monster ship plying the seas again by midnight - if they could get the overhead doors to cooperate.

High above, one man had climbed far out onto the second-level door to break the seal with a steel bar. In the control panel area a technician tried the switches by bumping them a bit at a time. The action unexpectedly jarred the man above. He struck his right hand with the prying tool and lost his grip, causing him to swing out into mid-air held from falling by his left hand only. His right hand was hurt beyond being of use to him and the crossing beams were too far away to grab with a foot. He shouted to those below.

"Help, I can't hold on!"

It gave Ningo an awful fright for he knew a fall was inevitable. Unlike the happy ending for Mark who was high over water when he fell, this unfortunate man was directly above yards and yards of hard dock planking. He looked around frantically for a way to break the man's fall.

*Attack of the Koto Maru*

Captain Matsumoto watched from the bridge, Naoki watched from a staircase he was descending, Paul and Susan watched from the tip of the bow where they had been involved with the anchor chains. Mark observed the emergency from the deck. All eyes were on the man with the fading grip except those of Ningo.

He raced to the side of the dock and grabbed a fistfull of escape netting stretched lazily between the ship and dock. A worker saw what he had in mind and ran over with a crane hook which was fortunately just lying there.

Ningo ordered a man into the crane cab. "Quick, stretch the rope netting as high as you can. We are his only chance!"

The hoisting crane popped a spark of ignition and soon rattled its ball-hook backwards toward itself. The netting, hastily fastened around it, slowly rose into the air making its way backwards and upwards in a spreading manner from the ship out over the dock. The ancient crane was a mass of spinning, clanking steel parts working together reluctantly. The sound of scraping metal and indexing ratchets pulled more netting close to its perfect position. Up went the captured end of the netting until it played taut with the end secured to the ship.

The dangling man held himself up on will alone. The blood had long since drained from his very last sinew. At last his grip failed. "Yaaaaa..." he yelled as he loosed his hand and streaked through the air toward the saving net.

After the acrobat landed safely in the wide-spread escape netting, the mood on the ship turned comical for he went rapidly back the way he came and did a flip. Upon landing the second time he broke into a giddy laugh which infected all who watched in fright. Eventually he came to stop. Ningo spun the net around and helped him off saying, "When tourists begin coming to the island we won't need a bungee jump. We have net jump!"

The needed mirth diffused what had become an insufferably intense decorum. Each individual went back to reviewing the drills in his own mind to make sure that if there were failure aboard the ship late tonight or tomorrow morning he personally would not be held accountable. Every motion must be flawless.

"Where do you want me during all this?" Paul asked.

"My father wants you to be out of harm's way in the bridge area along with Mark and Susan."

"Susan's going with us?"

"Heck yes," Susan yelled from the upper deck. She looked down at them and said, "You don't think I'd miss it do you? I want that little worm to see my face as he's captured!"

Paul admired the spunky woman but scratched his head and kept to himself a premise which was believed by most sailors of western nations. Evidently the Japanese didn't subscribe to the notion that it was bad luck to have a woman aboard a fighting ship. "Oh well," he mumbled. "We're only going to stop a wallowing container ship from sailing far, just long enough to radio the powers that be. What can happen?"

The beachcomber clicked away with a camera he had purchased from the settlement's modest store knowing that somewhere down the line the photos might be important. "Some incredible scenes, huh?" Mark offered.

"You bet! I'll need to illustrate my book anyway, and why not get some shots now? Each frame, with its depiction of real Japanese getting ready to sail a heretofore extinct World War II battleship into action will be a rare and unbelievable story. To today's reader whose memories of the great war are rooted in history books these shots may never be forgot!"

Mark smiled at Paul's enterprising nature and couldn't disagree with it. He went below to watch the men start the engines. Paul continued on his photographic odyssey speaking incidental mumblings to himself. Both men highly doubted that they would stay confined to the bridge area. There was too much to see.

"Here it is," the photographer thought, "a real situation, a real location in a hideout containing the ferocious bandits of the Pacific, making ready their slice of history from an island with a freakish cut through its middle. What a story!"

*Attack of the Koto Maru*

The sudden almost painful blast of ah-ooga horns knocked him from his concentration, and in fact almost made him slip off the dock toward the water.

"What's that!" he said as Susan passed by.

"I think the doors are opening."

Above the glistening decks of the <u>Koto Maru</u> and the teeming multitudes working there, a snapping groaning sound gave drama to the opening of the giant skylights. But the middle door seemed stuck. The hydraulic units continued to pull on the reluctant door warping the structural beams in a way no engineer could have intended. Everyone looked up and felt a collective anxiety grow in them as the pulling pounds of torque yanked mightily on the structure of the stuck door. The material of the door bent itself weirdly causing a popping, ripping sound just before the latch released with a heart stopping <u>Bang</u>! It was a noise which resounded off the walls and produced a small puff of bluish smoke at the latch. The worker who had fallen into the net grimaced holding his repaired hand. Some bits of dusty gossamer floated down as if they were pieces of the clouds themselves. The lower doors peeled away easily.

From within the island's gigantic cut the blazing stars, wondrous denizens of the deep night, couldn't easily be seen if the principal players in the cut had looked skyward. But the reliable residents of the heavens twinkled brightly this night as they have in countless millennia. Above the heads of the working islanders they seemed to beckon all humans to come out and play, out into their own cosmic presence and onward to the historic rendezvous a few earth miles away.

All the stars and planets gleamed as if they were diamonds on a tapestry monstrous in size and exquisite to the eye. Beams of reflection spattered in chops of wavy undulation off the waters surrounding the blue Pacific's tiny oasis of firmament - Timano. It seemed that all of heaven's celestial creations watched above the dark ocean for the <u>Koto Maru</u> to "arrive" into polite society and to make her, or his, first voyage as a finished ship.

*Alan De Wolfe*

But the friendly night sky hid all the sinister possibilities of real or imagined dangers. "Polite" may not have been the proper word for this debut and things that could go wrong quickly numbered in the hundreds. The mariners of Timano Island, plus three "extras" adjusted themselves for a center stage appearance in an early morning drama of fathomless consequence. Unfortunate was the fact, that in this same theater with its boundless stage all-hell was getting ready in the wings.

## CHAPTER THIRTEEN

Sometime in the same night, <u>Balboa</u> churned into the bay at Catena Island and heaved-to.

"This is about as close as we can get, Admiral Jessup."

"Looks okay to me, Captain. The off-loading boat should be here any minute."

"Just taking a little vacation, sir?"

"Er...yes. We'll take choppers out of here later."

Across the bay dim lighting could be seen on Catena Island and in a minute or two the small lights of a shore boat were seen closer than expected. Rear Admiral Jessup inquired of Captain Conlin, "Are you and the men coming ashore for the night?"

"No, I guess not, Admiral. The men are anxious to get on to Australia in our leaky old tub - just to get it over with. After that they get first class accommodations and a first class trip back. You know how it is."

An imperceptible sigh of relief mingled with Jessup's next words. "Yeah, I guess you're right."

"Let's see..." The captain checked his watch. "It's 12:01 A.M. now. We'll lay at anchor until just after dawn and then vamoose."

"Okay, Captain. Get a good night's sleep."

"Thank you, sir."

Under his breath Jessup mused, "It'll be your last!"

Jessup's guests came forward through the starboard companionway stepping out on deck as if relieved to be at anchor. All during the trip Captain Conlin had an uneasy feeling about them but figured the leaky old ship had put them on edge. Truthfully, the ship had everyone on edge including himself and he was pleased that the trip was more than half over. The Aussies could do whatever they wanted with the old battlewagon. He and his skeleton crew had had enough.

The captain yelled at the deck crane operator for no other reason than to do what was expected of him. "Get that crate over the edge, seaman!"

"Aye, Cap'n!" came the expected reply.

About eighty miles south-southeast of the Balboa, a lighted crack in the earth could be seen by any beast or machine flying over Timano Island. But just yet, no aircraft or satellite this evening would betray the presence of a mighty giant from the not-too-distant past. Momentarily, the Koto Maru, untested but ready in all aspects was about to make its first imprint on radar since perhaps, ever. It slowly moved forward for the first time in nearly fifty years.

"Watch that pile of ropes," Naoki shouted from his position above the multitude of sailors lining the deck on both sides. Just over a thousand men were aboard the Koto, give or take a few. Any boy or man who could go, wanted to. Some were the old mariners and some the "new" ones. Naoki judged they numbered more than enough to stop an unarmed container ship until the modern carrier with Admiral Ingram aboard could bring the Nimitz into the area.

Paul informed Naoki, "There are shore guns on that island, y'know."

"I think they will not shoot. It would be very foolish - we are well drilled," came the reply.

A cautious Paul added, "But you are not tested. And you're not thinking of shooting back, are you?"

Naoki smiled back understanding the warning with a twinge of introspection. He gave an evasive answer. "We are confident."

Captain Matsumoto decided to let his son bark orders from the bridge because English had become the language best understood by the young ones. Right now, no one had any other duty than to make sure the ship coasted cleanly out of its berth and between the menacing rocks, either side. From the doorway outside and high atop the boulders gaggles of children reveled

*Attack of the Koto Maru*

cheerfully, happy to be up way past their bedtime to watch the ship thunder out of its natural berth into the bay.

About halfway through the opening Captain Matsumoto gunned the engines a bit. "Helmsman! Be very, very careful on the starboard bow!" The pilot Tony, son of the original pilot who could not make the trip due to age shouted his "aye, sir!" and recalled the subsurface rocks he'd snorkeled around many times as a child and adult. "I know right where they are, sir!" In his mind he pictured being down in the rocks as the "big boy" went by, a thought that made him ponder and shudder. "Just think of being underwater when a ship of this size goes past!"

Size was indeed a factor and Captain Matsumoto knew it. One tiny miscalculation of space on either side of the Koto Maru could tear a huge hole amidships before the engines could hope to stop her. She was a bulky lady in port but a sports car on the open seas.

In the twinkling of an eye the whisper-quiet engines hummed past the awestruck wives and very old men standing along the dock. Pangs of excitement tittered along the nerves of the children whose giddiness had become more sober now. A cheer went up when the stern of the big ship glided past the perilous rocks and beyond the last submerged rock Tony had snorkeled around earlier yesterday. Tony himself heaved a heavy sigh as he guided the ship past the king-sized slab. He looked at Naoki and smiled, "Glad we missed it!"

Susan and Paul joined the captain and Naoki outside on the flying bridge to take a look back beyond the glistening prop-wash.

"It's like the earth gave birth," Susan said wistfully, staring at the bright-lit crack in the island. The girl from Cincinnati felt the throbbing deck under her feet thump just a little more than it had a moment before and figured it was the result of Captain Matsumoto's engine room urgings. The ships telegraph read: "Ahead one-half".

As the workers who stayed behind closed the giant doors, the exterior lights aboard ship blinked on nicely illuminating each stairway and deck. "What a sight!" Paul clicked a few more pictures he knew wouldn't develop properly and uttered, "I never friggin' imagined anything like this." He also realized that during a war tour, a dreadnought like this would never run on the high seas lit up like daylight but it was fun.

"Paul, why don't you assist whoever's on the radio? It can be a two-man job and the young man who's in there might be needing your years of experience."

"Good idea, Mark. I can't wait to see this radio!"

Mark's wisdom seemed apropos. Paul trundled off to the wireless shack just inside the ship located about fifty feet behind the wheelhouse.

"Come on, Susan, I'll show you the engine room."

Naoki chimed in quickly to stop him. "Mark, I want her to stay here - it's safer. Why don't you see if you can help out with the big guns down below."

"Guns?" he said half joking. "You're not really going to use them are you?"

The captain's spokesman said, "You never know."

Mark held a blank, surprised expression for a good half minute letting it eventually fade to resignation. Naoki had changed a little, he reckoned. He kept his contemplative thoughts to himself, hunched his shoulders and walked off.

Susan stood nearby and noticed Naoki's rather important grin. Her distinct impression was that he wanted her near him, which to her was not an altogether unpleasant thought on this night of a thousand dreams. Each man, and woman, aboard the steely gray vessel conjured up a special place in history for themselves and for the speedy ship as they raced resolutely toward an early-light rendezvous with destiny. Each "boy" felt his true manhood finally coming to the fore right in front of the fathers who before this had relied on ancient stories to tell their sons. Tonight they would all make a few memories together. Tonight and beyond.

About seventy miles ahead of them the old <u>Balboa</u> lay at anchor wallowing in the easy surf. At the rail, Captain Conlin watched a bright moon trail from the horizon to his ship in lazy lines of reflectance. He looked toward the island at the container ship in the safety of the docking area and was only vaguely interested in the flurry of loading activity. He was oblivious to the long dark bunker wall.

"She must be going somewhere tomorrow, eh Cap'n?"

The words of his first mate jounced his contemplation. "Kinda looks that way, Rob. It's gonna be hard to go from military ships to merchant ships. What are you gonna do after this trip."

"Just retire, I guess. You? Are you still planning on going to work for Transtar."

The captain looked back at the container ship in the distance and said, "Yeah, I'll be driving one of those big cows before long."

Both men sighed almost at the same time and leaned hard on their forearms. Without giving it voice, each wondered about the contents of the crates they dropped off this evening with Jessup and his mysterious guests. Jessup on the other hand was glad the deal had been done. On the island's loading pad he broke open one side of the box to show the contents to a waiting Ranar Moolong.

"There you have them - our best atomic detonators."

"Good, good!" Ranar exclaimed. "Alright men, get these on the ship! Put them in the secret spot."

Jessup's ill-got cargo was the last thing the ship was waiting to load. Everything else was onboard and ready for sailing. The crew had to tie down a few last items in case the seas came up but in about an hour, all would be ready. The time was 2:15 A.M.

Ranar announced, "Come to the house for your payment gentlemen."

In a princely gait, he took his position at the front of a caravan of golf carts ready to wind their way up a paved roadway to the highest point possible. After a bumpy ride, the carts turned into a cul-de-sac driveway at the house.

Resplendent chandeliers twinkled above the main doors which opened on electronic command as the small conveyances pulled up. The men were impressed with the house, but itching for their payment.

Ranar led Jessup and the three other procurers into a large room overlooking a helicopter pad near the rear of the house. He snapped his fingers at a new man who had replaced the unfortunate Freddie and said, "Get the suitcases!"

When the luggage was brought forth, the ultra-rich Ranar popped open one of them. Inside was the crispy green tender known so well in the world for the dreams it imparts to the owner - cash, and lots of it!

"Here you are, gentlemen. There's three million U.S. in each bag along with many feelings of heartfelt gratitude from the Sultanate of Malua. We shall all be, and remain, rich enough to get us through this life and the next. Thank you, very much!"

After Jessup and his cohorts pawed through the greenbacks for a moment Ranar spoke one last time. "Enjoy your sleep! The choppers will take you to your destinations tomorrow at daybreak. For now, goodnight and dream sweetly. Perhaps we will have another deal sometime."

A crescendo of cigar-chomping and back-slapping went on for the next few minutes as Ranar exited the room to get himself ready to sail aboard the big freighter. Jessup and his nefarious procurers allowed themselves to feel relaxed and rich, though they were still not off the island. Jessup was headed for Amsterdam to become anonymous and the other three wanted themselves and their money flown to the Isle of Man. In either place, the money would be safely away from the prying eyes of Uncle Sam and available to them at any time by wire. With so much money "offshore" they would never need to go to the U.S. again. Each would live as he desired for many, many years with no one to answer to. It was a dream come true.

"Hell," Jessup roared in laughter. "I just might go back to my job until I get the pension!"

*Attack of the Koto Maru*

Out in the bay, on the decks of the stoic <u>Balboa</u>, the well-lit balmy night showed a busy hum drum aboard the container ship. Workers walked to and fro concluding their loading duties.

The same bright night was considerably darker along the broad expanses of the bunker wall. The inky blackness hid some other workers, who were up very high on the concrete surface of the bunker removing concealment shrouds from the deadly shore guns. These sinister guns would finally see some action, come morning. No one on the <u>Balboa</u> saw the preparations, or knew of their deep consequences.

About forty miles away Captain Matsumoto turned it up a notch to assure a dawn arrival in the vicinity of Catena. The <u>Koto Maru</u> glided effortlessly through black waters slicing ahead with the precision of a surgeon's lancet. Except for the winds everything seemed very quiet. None of the young men expected the ship to be so quiet and smooth.

"My son."

Naoki, standing nearby on the bridge said, "Yes, father?"

"I have bad feeling about this. Go check the big guns and make sure of our readiness."

"Yes, sir!"

"Tell everyone not to hesitate when orders from the bridge are given."

"Yes, sir."

Down near the turrets Susan stood at the deck rail with Mark. She had left the bridge to get some of the rejuvenating air blowing past the ship in a hurry. The moonlight played with her fresh-smelling hair while racing breezes dashed it about like silk curtains. Mark's short haircut appeared not to move at all. He paused in his speech about ships.

"How do you feel about this, Susan?"

She turned her back to the speeding water, tossed her already tossed hair and sighed with gusto, "It's wonderful. I've never felt so happy to be alive!"

"Yeah, salt air will do that to you."

Mark was a guy usually under complete control of his emotions, but on this star-splashed night on the speeding Koto Maru he let himself be influenced by Susan's fatal radiance. The navy man planted a lingering kiss on her lips. He hadn't planned to, but it felt good.

Naoki rumbled down the ladder as the two broke their surprise lip-lock with a pop. A momentary expression of disappointment crossed his veneer but he smiled bravely and stepped quickly within the turret door. The two looked back at one another from a wide separation not entirely sure the kiss was a good thing. They talked in silhouette for nearly an hour against a splendid backdrop of lunar light and hoped they had not offended Naoki. Their monstrous battleship was more than halfway to Catena. Their emotions were unsettled.

# CHAPTER FOURTEEN

Moments before dawn, the Balboa came to life with a start of its engines. The captain yawned his way to the bridge and greeted his first mate. They hadn't slept long, but it was enough.
"Morning, Rob."
"Morning Cap'n. Wow, this stuff is strong!"
The first mate took his chewable coffee and left the pilot house stepping outside to the flying bridge. He yelled to the men forward at the bow. "Stand by at anchor!" Everyone aboard was anxious to get underway and on to Australia while the good weather held. The captain looked at the tall concrete walls with wonder, not having seen them the night before. He also wondered about the openings - like vertical slits - like a fortress. Thoughts of a soon-concluded voyage were on everyone's mind when the first loud boom pealed forth from Catena.

No one can remember exactly when the first puff of smoke appeared, but all members of the Balboa's skeleton crew would recollect it often over the next few weeks. It was sometime within the next five seconds that a searing projectile whistled through the early morning air, missing the bow by scant inches and blowing away a quiet awakening on the old tub. A dumbfounded first mate spit his cigarette off the flanking walkway and out over a good portion of water. He flung his coffee over the rail and yelled, "My God, someone's firing on us! It's coming from the island!"

Before a stunned Captain Conlin could put enough thoughts together, a second projectile mirrored its colossal explosion off his ashen face gouging its madness into a rear hatch. A resounding boom issued forth from the aft decking causing the ship to rock violently in the calm water. It sent a billowing black thunderhead hundreds of feet into the air.

Ah-ooga horns answered the ballistic barrage aboard ship with a frightening din of their own. The captain thought of the few men below decks. He shouted into the communications network. "All Hands on deck!"

The first mate followed with a futile order. "Uncover the guns!"

As a third shot was initiated from the island, all men from below raced out of various hatches bewildered and befuddled by the unexpected attack. Instinctively they ran to battle stations only to realize there were but two working guns with outdated fifty millimeter ordnance abounding. These were put into service as quick as possible after the third projectile impacted the front plates ripping steel and decking from the bow. The deck guns were soon found to be inadequate and were abandoned after a few thousand fired rounds. The inability of <u>Balboa</u> to fire back with proper arms made the thick concrete walls of Catena Island look even stronger. A frustrated captain felt anger replace surprise.

"Get away from the guns stations! Save yourselves!" came the order.

Smoke poured heavily up through the open holes where deck planking had been blown halfway to kingdom-come, most of which sailed over the control tower and very near the captain's head. Conlin ducked in time but smoke quickly claimed his space.

Coughing and hacking along the tilting stairwell he steadied himself with twisted beams of deck rail shouting his order to "cut the inflatable rafts loose!". The men all headed for the center of their dying ship to release the rafts and as many boats as possible. For now, they would float the boats off as the water rose to touch their bottoms. Later they would swim to them. They were now acting on instinct alone but tried in their own minds to make some sense of it all. A fourth projectile slammed into the bridge where a moment ago all had been serene in the early calm of morning. Not so now.

The ship was igniting from within, thanks to the fuel mixture in her belly and dazed but lucky crew members found themselves located on the opposite side of the maelstrom, away

*Attack of the Koto Maru*

from the exploding fury. Huge power blasts went through the starboard side after nearly all men had jumped off the port side into relative safety. Their God-awful coffee was completely forgot after imbibing a chaser of raw oil swirling all around them. It slicked the water with a shiny black goo and would soon burn their skin red. A swimming outing with their ship blowing up in front of them was the last thing the seamen thought they'd be doing this morning.

In the smoke and pounding explosions the ship could hardly be seen. A few boats bobbed in the choppy surf but no one had got into them yet. Through occasional openings in the smoke, the captain could see the island's giant concrete wall puffing off ordnance after ordnance along its entire length with unanswered abandon. The shells were coming fast and furious now and the men feared for their lives unashamedly.

"What are they doing!" Rob yelled inanely at the captain.

Captain Conlin reached up over the edge of a collapsible lifeboat and was helped aboard saying, "I think we've been set up! God knows why!"

As the ship began sinking on an even keel the barrage of shells diminished and stopped momentarily. The men stared at the old tub and wondered collectively what was next for them, and why had the shelling stopped? The captain thought, "Will boats be sent out to finish us off? Whoever perpetrated this evil act will have to finish the job lest the survivors reach safety and talk. And what did Jessup have to do with this mess?" The mood in the one rubber raft and one wooden lifeboat was of somber, desperate confusion. A couple more shattering broadsides hit the disappearing ship as men tumbled in to reclaimed lifeboats three and four.

Startled and amazed were inadequate words describing the captain's view of the surviving sailors. To his relief, it seemed they were all accounted for when he concluded a quick count. He and the struggling men didn't notice a force coming from behind them through early morning fog patches, but would soon register amazement for a second time on this very special day.

Deafening shells from the island had ceased to rain down. Island radars had sensed another presence riding high in the water on a tear toward their location, a presence with an unusual radar signature, a presence of dangerous and monstrous proportion. Their evil act within the walls of Catena Island had been well understood by the coming thunder. The reckoning force was not to be stopped, it was only to be puzzled over for a long and onerous moment.

Behind the thick walls, one of the shore gunners continued to look with puzzlement into his radar screen. Others gathered round buzzing in the silence of the battery guns.

The commander of the shore installation strode in with Rear Admiral Jessup, who had been joyfully watching the cruiser and her complement of witnesses sink in the estuary.

"Why have you stopped!" the commander quizzed.

One of the men said, "Something is coming!"

"Impossible!" Jessup returned. "There's nothing in this area! I checked it myself! And the <u>Nimitz</u> is still down."

In the distance a gigantic boom was heard directly behind the swimming men, late of the <u>Balboa</u>. A phantom dreadnought signaled its presence by firing one warning shot for all to turn their heads and see. The precursor from its huge forward guns indicated a willingness to do whatever was necessary in battle to win. It was a warning that said, "Give up or perish!"

The shore commander looked at the speck on the horizon from a position high atop his fortress and suddenly felt a twinge of vulnerability. Its radar imprint was massive - unlike anything except an aircraft carrier. "Is it a carrier?" he said vacantly.

The guns of Catena Bay which had begun the morning with an outrageous act of attempted murder might now be engaged in battle by a something not nearly as helpless as the old <u>Balboa</u>. The stage was set for Matsumoto's ethereal specter to roar in from the early morning mists, making its outdated radar signature bigger and bigger, looming suddenly and gigantically behind the backs of the stranded men.

*Attack of the Koto Maru*

"What the hell is that thing!" Rob shouted at the waterlogged captain.

As it drew nearer Captain Conlin exclaimed. "Galloping ghosts of World War II! Stay low, men!"

Captain Matsumoto purposely hurried past the stricken men in the water to put the ballistic shock wave ahead of the soggy swimmers. The <u>Koto Maru</u> burned past them by what seemed like inches before a mighty roar from the front turrets split the momentary calm of Catena Bay. The heavy projectiles agitated the waters ahead of them into jumping ripples of movement. The soaked captain and his wet companions had never seen the low-slung decks of a battleship go past them so close and so fast, nor had they seen any decks teeming with young Japanese in bright uniforms. Japanese?

Captain Conlin looked at the flying bridge and said incredulously, "Do I see a crew-cut American with a woman in the middle of a hundred Japanese? Are they waving? I must have swallowed too much of this stuff!"

Three deafening blasts from the eighteen-inch guns tore through the air in the direction of Catena's concrete edifices, followed by several blasts from the six-inch muzzles. The ship delivered huge ka-booms against the yielding concrete and men flew around in the acrid smoke inside like disoriented birds. As the <u>Koto</u> slipped by, Conlin spotted the "rising sun" stretched stiff by the wind and shouted, "It <u>is</u> Japanese! How the hell can it be Japanese!?"

Captain Conlin uncovered his eyes after two more thumping blasts and felt his mouth drop open. "It looks brand-new!" He and his shocked men bobbed in the wake of the speedy ship flipping and dipping in the unavoidable backwash. Conlin popped backwards out of the boat like a spring-loaded toy but didn't care. He was starting to like what he saw.

The off-rhythm of <u>Koto's</u> anti-aircraft guns added their pa-toom, pa-toom, pa-toom to the widening variety of sound, a sound that told the seasoned Conlin that Catena Island was now in dire straits and apt to get more than they gave the settling <u>Balboa</u>.

"See how those bastards like that! he yelled.

Watching the guns of Catena attempt to return fire he allowed himself an optimistic smile. "Thank God the island guns forgot about us!" The mystery ship was on a hit and run pattern throwing everything it had at the evil island excepting the galley utensils. The mighty walls of an evil stronghold began to crumble.

"Hard to port," Matsumoto asserted, noticing with pride the damage occurring in the concrete fortress. Naoki looked down out of the wheelhouse on the belching guns. They seemed to be coming from directly under his crotch. He felt only astonishment with no appropriate words. He and the other "boys" were in the midst of a war condition which one of the young men had once called "impossible". It seemed they were doing well. "What a rush!"

In the concrete edifice damage was indeed occurring. Jessup watched in horror as holes were torn easily in the massive walls of the enclave. The <u>Koto</u> was doing exactly what she was designed for.

"Get that thing," Jessup roared.

"It is impossible! It is moving too well!"

Close to a nearby hit, one of the gunners in the bunker went flying across the lab section where all had been peaceful only moments before. Shattered glass flung its shards in every direction right along with him. In front of his wide eyes Jessup ducked the glass and watched the airborne man splatter and stick briefly to the far wall. Ragged pieces of concrete wall held the man against itself for a moment like a Roman alto rilievo sculpture.

It was the last straw for the admiral. He was sorry he'd stayed around so long to watch the old <u>Balboa</u> disintegrate. Panic gripped him with both hands.

Matsumoto turned the ship in a run-away direction aiming his bow away from the island but making the stern perpendicular

*Attack of the Koto Maru*

to it. This maneuver kept the ship's silhouette narrow and gave his aft guns their turn to damage the high walls. Now it was time for the rear cannons to get in a few shots.

Susan and Mark were in one of two rear turrets standing near Ningo when the signal was given to fire. The guns screamed a series of explosive detonations which blasted their way through Susan's earplugs. The resulting vibration was a thing one could only experience on a ship like this, on this day, at this hour. The recoil of the big gunnery unit actually pushed the mighty ship ahead slightly. In reflex, Susan wailed a brief cry even though she'd known what to expect. "Just like a woman!" she stuttered, angry with herself.

The men of Catena were shooting wildly for they had not expected a moving target. "Like shooting pond fish," Jessup had said earlier. Now with the new danger from "whatever that thing is" Jessup could only think of getting out of there and saving his own skin. Not many men had been left on the island - just enough to finish off the <u>Balboa</u> and clean up the odds and ends. But now, the concrete walls were taking some disastrous hits and could reduce the number of men substantially.

Jessup took a last look through binoculars at the high-tailing ship and saw the Japanese flag. His shocked expression couldn't hide the fear. "I'm gettin' outta here! It's a damn ghost! Where are those pilots!"

Far in the distance, beyond the range of the shore guns Captain Matsumoto changed the silhouette of his ship again letting the early sun reflect off its turning side. In just a moment the bow came around to face the island of Catena once more and to put final destruction upon the tall evil walls.

From a distance, Matsumoto unleashed probably the greatest single volly of projectiles ever launched from a ship of this size. His reasoning made good sense.

"Well, it's the only time we can fire the shells."

"Yes. Let's get rid of them!" Ningo said, ecstatic.

The entire ship shook with kinetic energy. It began to forever lay waste to the fortress of a spoiled-child potentate bent on ruining the world. The huge blistering round of firepower suddenly came from the island but too short to damage the <u>Koto</u>. Matsumoto brought the ship around for a final run.

From a mile or two out, the <u>Koto's</u> engines heaved and throbbed and swelled to full power once again signalling the start of a final run to glory for the outdated but effective technologies riding above them. A massive push from the power plants stoked below by the sons of the original crew brought the seas behind the ship to a boil. The bow lightened itself in front of such an irresistable shove forward and trimmed the ship visibly higher up on the waves. Matsumoto figured that this time there was no surprise to the unfortunate men in the water. They had plenty of time to plug their ears. He telegraphed "full speed ahead" and put the spurs to his raging ship.

The bow wash climbed higher and higher on the bulkheads as the battlewagon came roaring into the bay. Every forward gun blazed with the sound of hell itself. A sudden slight turn lit up the side gunnery introducing even more noise to the caustic mix of madness. The wave from the knife-edged bow climbed high to the rail and blew mists off its top as the ship did a "skid" sideways. The fortress began to dismantle like the building blocks of a child.

Everything that could vibrate, did. Even the old <u>Balboa</u> rattled, sunk to its radar antennae and resting nearly out of sight on the bay floor. The men tied the boats to its upper structure and the swimmers clung to its wet metal. Dazed expressions washed across faces that flickered reflections from the flaming gun barrels. They watched the panorama of astounding gunfire go thundering past them with a pride not misplaced. Whoever, whatever that glorious ship was, the boys in the water were wholly behind it.

"My God what a sight," Conlin said, watching from behind the radar antennas of his sunken command. "Beelzebub himself would run from this ship! It's a helluva price to pay for a ticket, but I'm glad I'm here!"

*Attack of the Koto Maru*

On the Koto, Paul was trying to maintain his footing on a ship which shook and rattled strongly despite its like-new condition. He snapped photographs in a blur out the side door of the wireless shack while the young operator attempted to raise the Nimitz. He got a picture of Conlin and his wide-open mouth on the way past.

"The captain will love this one," he snickered. The radio operator's voice came in behind his.

"Nimitz. We are the Koto Maru. Are you there?"

Paul stepped back inside the radio shack where the din continued somewhat muffled. He spun the copying dials and said, "Okay, try this."

"Nimitz. This is Koto Maru"

After a moment of singing static the speakers crackled, "Koto, we have you. Why this frequency?"

"Our location is Catena Island. Come immediately"

After what seemed like a long time, the Nimitz replied, "This is Admiral Ingram. Are those your guns? We're coming your way but engines are at one half"

The Koto replied, "No big hurry. Thank you."

Miles away, Admiral Ingram put the microphone down. "Koto Maru? It can't be Japanese, they don't have guns like that anymore." He paused, held his breath and said, "Listen."

The Admiral looked numbly at the ceiling bulkhead with almost a reverent stillness as did most other officers in the immediate area. It was quiet except for the distant sound of thunder. Or was it thunder? Inside their "tin can", all they could do was look at one another.

"Send off a Corsair!" came the order.

Lieutenant Sheldon reminded Admiral Ingram, "Er...we don't have those anymore, sir."

"Well put something up, Lieutenant!"

Admiral Ingram wanted this development observed for posterity, and to cover his butt. "Get some pictures and report to me." It was only a moment before a speeding pilot lifted off from the big carrier on his way to observe the incredible.

*Alan De Wolfe*

On the flying Koto the sound wasn't very distant. Mark had begun helping out with the ordinance, having a great time reviewing things he'd only read about, kicking hell out of an unseen enemy, listening to their guns go silent one by one. Susan admitted defeat and cowered behind an inside ladder. On the bridge, Naoki shared the puffed up pride his father was feeling, knowing the Koto was finally something other than a centerpiece for the island. Through the smoking guns he scanned the coastline.

"Oh, no!" he said with alarm. His binoculars stopped their sweep at the loading dock. "The damned container ship is gone!"

Captain Matsumoto quickly looked eagerly only to conclude the same thing. He muttered some unintelligible Japanese and telegraphed "reverse engines".

The speeding warship slowed amazingly under the feet of a disbelieving Mark Ingram. "Holy cow, the brakes work!"

After a long slowing arc, the ship calmly diminished itself to a crawl and cruised sedately, completing a circle near the sunken Balboa. The war with Catena Island was over with some last explosions trumpeting within the shambled walls. Pieces of the wall blew outward like one last oozing sore. Only the scars of death remained.

Everyone breathed easier watching the main wall collapse into itself with clouds of dust. Each person aboard quickly appeared on deck cheering in island chants and Japanese phrasings except the American guests. The placid waters of Catena Bay had stopped churning and were now conducive to putting boats in. After a time the men of the old Balboa, some still attached to the upper structural beams of their sunken ship, were picked out of the tepid waters. Everyone on the stopped ship watched as the Balboa crew were brought over and piped aboard.

The flabbergasted Conlin and his men finally climbed aboard via the starboard ladder, forming themselves into a silent line amazed at the profusion of Japanese uniforms. Equally

*Attack of the Koto Maru*

amazing were the sloe-eyed faces quietly peering back at them without malice, without expression, without talking. Conlin contemplated a major case of goose bumps in the weird quiet and decided to wait to speak. Each side stood lined up looking at the other awkwardly for quite some time as they all waited for the captain.

Matsumoto descended the stair ladder from above and said, "Welcome to the Koto Maru, gentlemen. We did not plan to come in shooting but our telescopes told us it was necessary. We have some dry clothing for you below and some welcome shower units." Naoki spoke up from amongst the smiling younger members, "Yes, and you are not prisoners of the Japanese Imperial Navy!"

Able to hold their cool no longer, everyone from Timano reacted with the side-splitting laughter of adolescence including the captain, who was more relieved every minute that he didn't have to conceal the Koto any longer. "We are just the proud owners of an old antique."

Mark, Susan and Paul introduced themselves to the stunned Conlin but very quickly got back to business. Mark told him, "Captain, we'll explain it all later but right now we have business to attend."

Paul shouted, "Look!"

On the smoking island, a line of men stood at the loading dock with hands behind their heads in a surrendering pose.

"Let's get to shore. We have a few questions to ask and we have to do it fast."

The captain's launch was already over the side with engines starting easily as if they were new, which they were - almost. The launch boat had never been off the ship nor had it touched sea water before today. After the men piled on, the power boat performed to perfection as they expected, dashing the men quickly to Catena and to the hapless gunners waiting for their own arrest. All young men on the Koto were thrilled to know the taste of war their fathers had always talked about. At the same time, the old men felt their renewed youth mingle with the young ones.

When they arrived on the island Paul and Susan stepped off the boat last. To Susan, her fourth trip to the island was much better than the first one. Paul was just glad the whole thing was over. The container Susan arrived in was still exactly where she had left it, with rubber tire marks still scorched on its interior floor. "This is where I came in," she thought.

"Where is the ship!" Mark yelled at the bunker's gunnery commander.

The man hesitated until the American flew in anger. "I said where's the damned ship!"

The thickly accented voice showed its surrender. "It departed early, about 4:30 A.M."

"And Jessup?" Mark scowled.

"By helicopter, about twenty minutes ago. Going to Schiphol."

Mark was angry and frustrated that this boss of his whom he trusted for several years was in on a deal to arm other countries - countries having no appreciable moral fiber nor compassion for anyone. "Oh hell! I can't let the rat get away! But how do I get to Amsterdam?"

As he said his words aloud, the gigantic <u>Nimitz</u> blew its whistle from the southwestern horizon.

# CHAPTER FIFTEEN

"Yes!" Paul hooted.

He watched his neglected skiff being towed by one of the motor launches from the <u>Nimitz</u> in the direction of the mother ship's giant fantail. Along with the big house on top of the hill, his little boat had survived the murderous shelling and would now find itself attached to one of the biggest ships afloat. "Safe!" he thought. The bunker, which a mere two days ago had looked so strong, was leveled into dust and partially-standing walls. It continued to smoke, its contents being sifted through by U.S. sailors, its tennis court painting skewed like a pretzel.

When things calmed down later, Admiral Ingram greeted the group in his quarters. "What in tarnation was this all about, Mark?"

Mark looked at the improbable gathering of Admiral Ingram, Paul, Susan, Naoki, Ningo and Captain Matsumoto and explained it to the best of his histrionic abilities. But he also did it briefly because a certain ex-Rear Admiral Jessup was still on the run and Mark didn't want the trail to get cold. He let it be known quickly and took his story to its conclusion.

"So you see, uncle, I've got to get to Amsterdam fast. And I'd like Susan and Paul to go along..."

"And Naoki!" the islander shouted.

"Er...well, yes, maybe that's a good idea. That way we can spread out more," Mark added.

"Get to the point, Lieutenant."

"Well, if Jessup gets his money in some bank in the Netherlands, we may never get hold of it. The commander of this smoldering bunker told me his suitcase had three million bucks in it, not to mention the sums the other three got away with. The other men went to the Isle of Man presumably to use the impregnable banking system there. Maybe we can get them, maybe we can't, they left a lot earlier. But I think we can surprise Jessup if we hurry."

*Alan De Wolfe*

The admiral pushed back in his chair and thought. "That rat! I never thought he'd be capable of this." The room went silent. The admiral contemplated further.

"Okay, here's what we'll do. We'll get you to Kwajalein in the Marshall Islands, which is almost due west of here, and have some commercial transportation standing by. If you leave from Kwajalein I think you can get to Schiphol airport ahead of him. The island base is the only place nearby with flights going in that direction except for maybe, Indonesia. I'll pull some diplomatic immunity so you won't have to have passports with you. That's all I can do. Thank God I'm an admiral!"

"I'm sure that'll do it, sir."

The admiral stood up and sighed. "Now all I have to do is tell Washington our engines are down again, that I just watched an island blow up, that I'm going to arrive in Japan for the disarmament conference on a World War II Japanese battleship after I stop a container ship full of atomic devices! Could you make it a little more believable next time?"

Paul inserted, "Tell the captain of your fabulous flattop to be careful with my little boat, eh, Admiral?"

"We'll see if it'll fit in the aft seawell."

Paul, Susan, Naoki and Mark stayed together and found time for a brief snack aboard the big ship only moments before their chopper ignited its engines. Naoki jumped into some donated clothing. The others were dressed well enough in casual attire, intending to cop some different duds in Amsterdam as opportunities presented themselves. It wasn't supposed to be a vacation. They would fend for themselves as best they could.

"Susan, I thought you wanted to see the sultan's expression when he was captured." Paul chided. "If you do, you'll have to remain on the Koto while the crew tries to catch the container ship."

"And miss the expression on Jessup's face? Never! I want to ask Jessup how he'd feel if he were kidnapped off the friggin' beltway and shipped in a container halfway 'round the world!

*Attack of the Koto Maru*

Believe me, he's going to get a piece of my mind. I'd like to be on a bus with him for about fifteen fire-breathing minutes!"

After a warm-up the pilot signaled for them to board the chopper, making sure they were properly cautioned about the extreme high air turbulence around the craft. The travelers emerged from the base of the control tower and scurried heads down across the rough carrier surface toward the big airship. Susan was last to climb aboard peering through a comical tangle of hair. Her rapport with these three traveling companions was great, and good thing. Sometimes the humor hovered on the brink of irritation.

"Your hair is beautiful, Susan." Naoki snickered, helping her aboard with strong, tanned arms.

"Shut up, dirt bag." she countered, amusing everyone. Naoki flashed a luminous grin and giggled impishly. Somewhere in her manner he saw a glint of sweetness. He knew it was aimed at his heart, or at least he hoped so. She gave him a long look, not wishing to escape his grasp. All three men felt a rekindled warmth for her at the same moment, but Naoki's interest smoked.

The chopper lifted off at the same time Admiral Ingram, Captain Matsumoto and Ningo headed for a launch to take them off the Nimitz and over the sea about a quarter mile to the Koto Maru. Matsumoto didn't expect to have an admiral onboard his ship and also didn't expect to continue his pursuit.

But it was necessary to stop the container ship and the nefarious Ranar Moolong before their cargo could be sold to suspicious countries. The Koto was well fueled and aware of the escaping ship's location, thanks to the glib gunnery commander captured only an hour ago. Matsumoto thought, "God knows, all the world needs now is a few loose bombs to make it more unstable than it is already! And how ironic, a Japanese ship in pursuit of A-bombs!"

Admiral Ingram cut into the captain's reverie by asking the two rescuers all about their ship and how they'd managed to keep such a secret from the world. With them, he stepped into the launch and caved-in to his curiosity. "I can't wait to board that baby!"

On their way to the Koto the admiral said, "What a wonderful opportunity to view history!" The remark brought a puff of pride from Matsumoto and his young gunnery officer. Ningo himself could hardly wait to see the admiral's expression when he was piped aboard the Koto and found himself highly outnumbered by Japanese uniforms.

While the Nimitz stayed behind to get her engines ship-shape and study the destroyed fortress more closely, the Koto once again throbbed to life and throttled up to apprehend the much slower container ship. The engines churned-up, the radio crackled and the Koto Maru dashed majestically out of Catena Bay. A lot of American sailors made a lot of entries in their journals that evening.

The freighter's destination was Singapore. All men who go down to the sea in ships knew that the steamy Asian port of Singapore is a mighty difficult place to keep track of a freighter, or at least, its cargo. The city's harbor is visited by ships of all registries, sizes and colors. If a crew really wanted to fool their pursuer, a needle in a haystack could be found more readily than a piece of cargo from a ship in Singapore harbor.

It was hoped that the Koto's superior speed would intercept the freighter well before Singapore. After obviating Ranar and placing him in custody, the Koto planned to proceed to Tokyo harbor and deliver the admiral to the arms reduction conference. No doubt, today's Japanese would be amazed by the big gray warrior and already Admiral Ingram was talking about having the conference aboard the big ship. It would be a way of drawing attention to his conference, a way of getting the biggest bang for his buck. He liked it.

This situation was made-to-order for an admiral who fully realized what a friendly press could accomplish as far as garnering support and free publicity for this timely conference was concerned. His personal commitment was to get atomic bombs outlawed forever with considerable attention given

*Attack of the Koto Maru*

toward getting rid of chemical warfare also. He knew the wheels of the world press were already turning out positive copy regarding the amazing Koto Maru. The resurrection of the ship and subsequent capture of a madman with a bunch of bombs, was a public relations gift from God. After the mid-ocean capture of this maniac from Malua, even Singapore would breathe a lot easier. The Koto got on about its business.

Ranar had smaller freighters standing-by in Singapore harbor waiting to dispatch the bombs to their final destinations. Such a thing could not be allowed. Thanks to a shiny new fifty-year-old battlewagon full of men who were somewhat Japanese and their guest one feisty American admiral, it was likely that Ranar's heyday was nearly finished.

But the other arm of the chase - Jessup - was another story. In the noise of the chopper Paul asked Mark, "What's the plan?" Mark shuffled in his jumpseat to get closer to the other three. "Jessup can't get to Amsterdam before us, it's just logistically impossible. I imagine he'll go to a spot with commercial service and take a plane, like we have to, and will ditch his naval uniform. It's anybody's call as to exactly which spot he'll choose but I'd guess somewhere in the Solomon Islands or Indonesia. He couldn't go to any of the American protectorates over here because he wouldn't risk having someone spot him."

"I wouldn't count on that." Paul interjected.

"By now this incident has been put on the airwaves. Everyone will be watching for him. But he's clever and bold. We should expect anything."

"On the airwaves" was a good guess. While the four helicopter passengers were on their way to the island of Kwajalein, news of the Japanese phantom ship was crackling from island to continent faster today than was ever possible in the day of the giant ship's construction. Japanese news service organizations and tabloids jumped in with all boilers glowing quickly turning the propellers of communication with great speed.

*Alan De Wolfe*

Up to the minute accounts were being solicited from the Timano islanders who could never have fancied a more sensational response to their decision to turn the <u>Koto Maru</u> loose. The high seas of imagination gripped the ears of the world press with a fabulous breaking story in which the word "sensational" was hardly adequate. The <u>Koto</u> chased the freighter, Mark and crew chased old Jessup, and soon the ravening press would chase them all. Paul figured their group still had a little time before the press began getting in the way. He busily made notes for his planned book.

Unfamiliar as the woman was with actual naval operations, Susan pled guilty to ignorance and asked, "So Mark, what is a Kwajalein?"

Mark smiled and tried to put his voice above the noisy chopper. "Kwajalein began as a sleepy atoll in the middle of the Pacific. During World War II the Japanese established a base and airfield there after taking it from Germany. How they did that I don't know exactly, but it was of great importance as the war escalated. The U.S. captured it towards the end of the war and made it a naval base."

"We held onto it after the great war and made it into a missile testing range. It's pretty well-developed these days and people who have to be stationed there are quite happy with it. It can be hotter than hell and rain is abundant, but there is great beauty in the physical presence of the reefs. As you may know, an atoll is a collection of reefs forming a circle. Kwajalein's reefs are shaped in a giant slanted ring. The reefs have grown almost completely around the lagoon which is about 190 miles in circumference. In another millennia, they probably will."

"Only one of the southern reefs is big enough to establish an airstrip and everything else is pretty much located there too. The lagoon incidentally, is the largest in the world."

"Sounds nice," Susan remarked.

"It isn't bad at all. The population is a little over seven-thousand I believe. They signed a free-association compact with the U.S. in 1982. That makes them self-governing. The people

*Attack of the Koto Maru*

are mostly micronesian and some are polynesian. They seem to maintain good rapport with the U.S. and their main product is anything related to coconuts."

"So I take it we can get a jetliner there," Paul offered.

"Yes, but we'll probably have to stop once in Tokyo or Jakarta, then on to Amsterdam and Schiphol airport."

Paul piped up again. "Speaking of Jakarta, I read an account of the day the Krakatoa volcano blew itself apart in 1883. A Dutch vulcanologist named Van Gestle was on a neighboring island studying the impending eruption when he was knocked flat and unconscious by the shock wave. The sound was heard in Australia and the resulting tsunamis were the highest in recorded history."

"Judging from our wave a few days ago, I would have hated to be around for that show!" Susan said.

Paul hastened to add, "I'll second that!"

While the crew and guests on the helicopter sped along toward the tiny speck of Kwajalein atoll vibrating to the discordant noise of a humming turbine engine, Admiral Ingram was having the time of his life watching the Koto pursue the freighter. From the radio shack, where he listened to transmissions from unbelieving U.S. naval captains to a tour-de-force lecture on outmoded battle capabilities, he paraded around the phantom ship with Captain Matsumoto to view all the perfect working machinery. He remembered the stories of the three sister ships and lamented their total loss, but now, here he was, walking on a near-duplicate of Japan's most celebrated warship ever, the Yamato. It was almost too much to cope with. Even for an admiral.

"This battleship is a treasure, Captain! What are you planning to do with it?"

Matsumoto stopped his tour of the turrets and pondered. "I think we will give it back to Japan. It will be a wonderful relic and could be a good museum for posterity. I'm sure there can be a place for it in Tokyo Bay or in the maritime museum."

"Oh, God yes! The Japanese of today will eat this up!"

The captain was interrupted from his predication by Ningo yelling down from the bridge. "Ship on the horizon, Captain...dead ahead!"

Admiral Ingram marveled at the way a rather old Matsumoto climbed the ladders leading to the bridge. He struggled to move his own out-of-shape body upward and thought, "Now for the pure fun of terrorizing an unarmed enemy!"

# CHAPTER SIXTEEN

Kwajalein was exactly as Mark described. Paul was accustomed to the heat and Naoki liked the humidity, but Susan was looking like a wilted rose. Naoki was mildly shocked at the air-conditioned comfort of the supermarket interior.

"It's cold in here," the islander said through his chattering teeth. The others were amused watching his arms and legs turn into rough planes of bumpy skin. "Don't ever go to Washington in January," Susan quipped.

"No kidding?"

"Yes. I'll wager you won't want to stay in the U.S. after living in your island paradise."

Naoki then tried to give her a little hint. "You should live on my island. You'd like it."

"Hmmm...I'll file that for later consideration."

Mark continued to sketch out their present location. "This store is pretty complete and I think they've got...yes, over there."

He led the little band left in the big store to a spot where the clothing racks were laid out in long lines. Susan was the first to tinkle the wire hangers, being immediately absorbed into a shopping technique nurtured by many years of U.S. living and a carte blanche spending permit from Admiral Ingram. In her mind, the store, and probably the whole island had all things necessary to help the troops stationed here feel right at home. The clothing was good, almost better than she'd remembered from Washington and the stores located in countless malls along the beltway. She almost forgot where she was.

An astonished Naoki couldn't believe the assortment before him. He ducked in and out of various racks of bright styles occasionally betraying his naivete with "wowie". This was going to be a landmark spending spree for an islander with absolutely no taste in western clothes whatsoever. With the cash provided by Uncle Sam he proceeded to buy far too much clothing and was assisted by Susan, who unabashed found herself caught up in his frenzy as well as hers. She was happy to watch him have his fun among the racks of clothes but far happier to be away from "his nibs", the ungracious and misguided Ranar Moolong. The whole situation played in and out of her thoughts as Paul and Mark confronted the shoppers with the one new item they would need to continue their journey - luggage.

"Don't spend too much time shopping, we have to get some food yet then get on the plane in about an hour and a half."

Mark and Paul were also delighted to watch Naoki lose himself amid all the clothing and other items in the big store. The islander had never seen a supermarket with food items, clothing and even a small restaurant they would soon be visiting all under one roof. It was great fun for an overgrown kid and everyone viewed the pack-rat side of Naoki with humorous introspections of their own.

Within a few minutes, Mark bit into a sloppy hamburger and spoke through the slobber. "It's just as I thought. The A-300 Airbus we'll be riding will stop first in Tokyo then proceed to Schiphol Airport in Amsterdam. I hope we're in time, though I don't honestly see how Jessup could get there ahead of us. When we get to Amsterdam, I think if we find out which flights are coming in from the Pacific islands we'll be able to watch the gates and nail the old man as he arrives. Since we have four people, it should be simple enough."

Paul handed everyone a small package and said, "Here. I picked up four London police whistles in the novelty section. When one of us sees Jessup at Schiphol, he or she must alert the other three. If the gate is too far for the whistle to be heard, stop him any way you can."

"Yes, he must be stopped," Mark added. "What are you going to do with all those clothes, Naoki?"

"I will send them back on the chopper when it goes. The pilot said he will get them to Timano somehow if I will invite him to come and visit. I did."

Susan queried with a coy grin, "Will I be invited back?"

*Attack of the Koto Maru*

"Only as my wife," Naoki glowed with a toothy smile.

The awkward silence Naoki caused with his calculated humor gave way to the necessities at hand. Susan "ahemed" her throat, being a little embarrassed by Naoki's weird proposal, then dismissed it not completely from her mind. The foursome adjourned from the snack bar and headed out into the early evening light.

The horizon was flat as a mirror and the sunset nearly perfect augmented with all the usual pollutions from mankind's abuse of the earth. Balmy evening air was far preferable to a day of nearly direct sun. Kwajalein's location, about nine degrees above the equator is a fact impossible to ignore.

In a little while, Mark went off to chat with an old friend he met outside the market and Paul walked down the beach as he had so many times in his immediate past. Susan quickly joined him and the conversation was light.

"Well, at least we made it off that wretched rock island, Susan."

The girl from Cincinnati replied through a wistful gaze, "Yes, without swimming. And I still can't believe I was nearly part of a harem! Sure am glad you came along." She softened her glance, "Thanks a lot, Paul. If it hadn't been for you..."

Paul lofted a big arm and squeezed her all around. "Think nothing of it, my dear. I could never have left you in that situation. It is odd that I happened to be anchored on Catena at just the right time. God puts us where he wants us. You see? He was looking out for you."

"How sweet," Susan thought. "What a nice guy!" Those womanly feelings of being taken care of felt delicious to her in the salty breezes of the island shore. She engaged Paul with the easy banter good friends use to assuage one another and continued to count her blessings. Not only had she been rescued by a Sir Galahad in a bathing suit, but she'd met a handsome lieutenant and a devastating islander too. In her mind she knew she could have her pick of these gentle guys, these men of fine manner and noble cause. Somewhere in the back of her thinking their very presence triggered the notion which pervades everyone's mind sooner or later - to settle down and love someone. This was a nice moment in her life. She relished it and let it mellow while the very last rays of sunset extinguished themselves in the water's distant horizon. She thought sleep would come easily tonight on the aircraft.

Over at the chopper pad, Naoki could be seen chatting away to the pilot of the <u>Nimitz</u> helicopter. Mark looked across the way and surmised he was busy telling the pilot to handle his new clothes with care. "That pilot will be very impressed with the hospitality he gets on Timano," Mark smiled calmly to himself. "He might even end up married." On Mark's right side, the giant Airbus rumbled into sight in preparation for its flight to Tokyo then Amsterdam. Naoki noticed it and bade farewell to the pilot.

In a half hour's time, a line of fifty or sixty people queued-up on the tarmac for entry into the metal cylinder meant to carry them to their various destinations. All stood at the Airbus with the sober expressions of assumed patience waiting too long as always for the ground crew to fling wide the doors.

When boarding began, the line of people looked very much like every other line ever seen waiting for a plane. There were several young couples heading out for a holiday in Tokyo, a businessman complete with suit and lap-top computer, a matronly older woman with an enormous hairdo and God-awful makeup, an old man with a scruffy beard and bushy eyebrows, a young bachelor heading for Amsterdam to do some "window shopping" and numerous uniformed servicemen going home to the U.S. via Asia and Europe. At the very end of the line stood Susan, Naoki, Paul and Mark. In the slow moving shuffle Paul announced his dread.

"I really don't like to fly," he said absentmindedly. "It's gotta be the fact that I'm not the one in control."

"These big babies have a very good record," Mark added.

"You still can't pull over and park if something goes wrong," the former businessman asserted. "I'd rather be sailing."

*Attack of the Koto Maru*

On the plane at last, Susan and Mark took their seats in front of the wing just ahead of Naoki and Paul. Paul plopped into a window seat behind Mark's elbow. Seat belts snapped closed throughout the passenger area, <u>No Smoking</u> signs popped on and the engines whistled higher for departure. The giant aircraft began its motion away from the terminal toward the taxiway with moderate speed giving everyone a last look at the encampment of Kwajalein. Evening lights twinkled on here and there as if to say good-bye to the lumbering metal monster.

The runway's east end was the beginning spot for a western takeoff. It had its back edge located at a group of commercial hangars not readily seen from the terminal building. Paul, ever curious, looked the buildings over very well when the giant craft rounded the taxiway to enter the main runway. There was no hesitation in the taxiing speed because no other aircraft were readying for takeoff. The engines sang out their high-tech crescendo like an ear with a severe case of tinnitus. Paul almost missed seeing the unlit chopper nearby. It piqued his interest and he strained to see.

The odd looking helicopter was black and shiny, just sitting there partially bathed in light from a nearby hangar. The darkened hangar behind the whirlybird had no logo on it but the chopper itself certainly did.

"Hey!" Paul said in a forced whisper.

The other three looked out the window at his urging, just in time to see the helicopter with <u>Sultanate of Malua</u> painted on its side.

"Oh no!" Mark exclaimed quietly, looking back between the seat and window at a stunned Paul. He gave Paul a long look and said, "Do you suppose...?" The two sitting beside them stretched over to take a look. "What does this mean?" Susan wondered aloud.

"Keep your voice down!"

Mark, trying to quell his own fear offered an explanation. "It means somebody we've all come to know could very well be on this airship right now!"

*Alan De Wolfe*

All four looked at each other blankly. Each then surreptitiously peered fore and aft in the plane's interior, eyes as big as dinner plates, wondering if they would be the one to spot something important. All four anticipated the troubles ahead with their own particular apprehension.

"It's very possible Jessup's on this craft!"

Susan cringed. "And I just had to come!"

"Now, we've really gotta get clever," Paul lamented, feeling a rekindling of his own airplane fears. "Who knows what this guy might do."

Mark sat around in his seat and recanted an old cartoon interrogative, "Now what, monsieur pussycat?"

Almost two hours previous to Mark's quizzical phrase on the speeding aircraft, in a different place, and on a much different vehicle Captain Matsumoto spouted some appropriate words of his own. "Fire number one!"

Just outside on the <u>Koto's</u> flying bridge, Admiral Ingram looked down over the big forward guns. One of them issued a deafening shot, exiting through a muzzle aimed straight ahead over the bow of Ranar's freighter. His weathered face squinted to fit binoculars into his eye sockets. He'd braced both legs without realizing it. The gun's smoking recoil stood his hair on end.

"Damn! I love it!"

Matsumoto glanced through the window at the gleeful U.S. admiral and puffed himself up again with pride. "How nice to have an admiral along to impress, one who looks like a child with a new toy." His prideful thought and his beaming smile carried right along with him as he stepped outside.

"Y'know, Captain," the admiral began, "I'm supposed to be going to a disarmament conference where we'll no doubt discuss the evils of smart bombs and heavy weaponry, but I can't help loving these amazing guns of yours."

"You are one of few to ever hear them, Admiral."

The two navy men shook hands lingering in one another's grasp in genuine warmth. The mutual gesture helped bring the

*Attack of the Koto Maru*

captain to terms with his long-standing unfulfilled feelings regarding the Second World War and the fact that the upstart U.S. Navy won hands down. For him, his amazing ship in its obvious perfection seemed to bring the spirits of all Japanese men killed in the war, and indeed, the Americans, into the light of modern understandings. In effect, it reconciled and transposed the desperate music of those souls drowned so long ago in this very ocean into a modern harmony impossible for either of them to describe with mere words. A simple handshake with a former enemy seemed to set it all straight and both men felt it. Both could see the mist in the other's eyes as he looked through his own. Words weren't necessary but they said them anyway.

"I'm not an insensitive man, my Captain."

"Nor I, my Admiral."

"Let us always be friends."

"We shall."

In silence, Captain Matsumoto turned slowly and strode back into the wheelhouse. The container ship riding beside them had not slowed as expected and the captain ordered another shot across her bows, this time closer.

Boom! came the report of a big forward gun. The admiral continued to watch the operation from the outside bridge deck appreciating every minute to the hilt and trying to keep his hat on in the brisk Pacific zephyr. Seldom had he felt so good, or so young.

By the time the freighter finally gave up the sun had barely sunk below the horizon and daylight still had some punch to it. Matsumoto brought the menacing presence of the Koto Maru to a crawl and then to a stop alongside Ranar's ship. He warmed up the electric megaphone, handed it to Tony and displayed a wink to the admiral. "What now?" Ingram wondered. The very good English of helmsman Tony rattled from the bridge window.

We are the Koto Maru of the Japanese Imperial Navy. You will surrender and prepare to be boarded. You must cooperate or we will blow you out of the water, sucker!

*Alan De Wolfe*

The admiral, still on the flying bridge, laughed till he roared when Tony's modern phrasing made Matsumoto smile. Through the panes of glass he yelled loud enough for the helmsman to hear, "I'll bet you couldn't wait to say that!" Still inside, the captain and Tony beamed a smile simultaneously and nodded approval. The slowing merchant ship pitched and tilted gently atop the calm megagallons of seawater beneath it and finally stopped.

Under the surprised scrutiny of Ranar's binoculars, boats were put in the water for the men of Koto, and its Nimitz guests, to cross over and board the container ship. Together they would secure it for the long trip to Tokyo harbor. The two stopped ships were finally side by side in placid water about six hundred yards from one another.

But the situation was suddenly more than a frustrated and angry future potentate could bear. From a wing deck at the aft end of the container ship, Ranar grabbed his automatic gun and attempted to spray the debarking Koto crew with machine gun bullets.

Though too far away to do much damage, Captain Matsumoto knew that the flash of princely fury manifesting itself in a hail of reckless bullets had to be answered with an indelible statement. His prearranged order came into play.

"Fire number seven!"

The crew below in the port side turret had been waiting all day to use their guns and in a second or two sent three volleys exploding toward the neighboring ship. The close proximity of the shock waves knocked the men on the freighter down like pins in a row. Concentric strata of smoke rings followed the projectiles in their trajectory whistling high above Ranar's head finding their mark in one of the highest containers on the deck. The container blew cleanly off the top layers of units, falling harmlessly beyond the ships middle and off the opposite side. Awash in blue smoke, Ranar immediately thrust his hands in the air to surrender.

*Attack of the Koto Maru*

Even his ego could not deny the truth, for if the Koto unleashed its firepower with vigor, every plank and seam in the freighter would open wide to the seas. The high-powered Koto could have taken the merchantman apart piece by piece, rivet by rivet. Seeing the Japanese captain and the American admiral together was enough to make Ranar Moolong reconsider his defiant stand and show signs of surrender. His capitulation lay bitter in his stomach.

"Now, that's more like it." The admiral said with a tiny laugh, still leaning his elbows on the rail.

After the men from the Koto and the company from the Nimitz had boarded the captured ship, Ningo saw to it that the search was thorough. The men had easily found the place where the bombs were kept and it was plain to see the detonators were not in place. It appeared that one end of each bomb, the end which held the detonator, was as yet incomplete with wiring hanging out and the systems obviously not connected. Owing to the fact that the islanders from the Koto and the sailors from the Nimitz would not have know what a detonator was if it bit them on the shin, it was assumed that the beaten Ranar was telling the truth when he said, "We have not purchased the detonators yet." It would take many days to thoroughly search the ship's nooks and crannies. Jessup had recommended a very good hiding place.

*Alan De Wolfe*

# CHAPTER SEVENTEEN

Flight 712 rumbled ever upward through a mucky Kwajalein sky made even darker with the approach of night. The steel cylinder kept its eventual rendezvous with the stratosphere and nosed itself down into level flight content with thirty-two thousand feet. In a minute or two, flight attendants unsnapped their seat belts and carried on with their preparations in the galley looking bored as always, making eye contact with no one.

Six seat-rows behind Paul, the man with the bushy beard and eyebrows rattled a newspaper holding it anxiously between him and the woman across the aisle whom he thought was staring. The woman with the gigantic hairdo sat across the aisle and could see him easily. No passengers sat between them. The flight was sparse.

"We have to get a good look at everyone," Mark said quietly. "If Jessup's on this plane, he's not gonna look like himself." The others agreed. Susan spoke.

"I'm first!"

In the European-built Airbus, the bathrooms are oddly located in a semi-circle around the very back of the tail section. Susan never liked the arrangement because the windows are at thigh-level. It made her uneasy to view clouds from that angle. Today she reckoned it wouldn't matter.

On her way to the bathrooms she would be able to look at everyone and see if Jessup was indeed on the flight. She knew very well what he looked like though it had been quite a while since she'd seen him up close.

Mark contemplated Susan's enthusiasm knowing she was not a woman to be left out of the action. "Okay, go ahead. But watch yourself. If he's here and if he's seen us, which must be true by now, desperate things will go through his mind. No telling what he'll do. We can't let him know that we know."

Paul realized that the dread he felt earlier must have been an omen. He smiled to himself and shook his head in resignation thinking of Dorothy Parker's witful insight at one of the old hotel round table meetings: "What fresh hell is this?" The next scene would begin with Susan's move.

She rose and slid into the aisle walkway. Susan moved slowly toward the back of the airplane walking behind an old woman with a cane. The lack of speed provided a lingering look at each person sleeping or reading or chatting with spouses or doing all things people do under the soft reading lights above them. She passed a doe-eyed navy man stroking his chin sitting askew in the seat and looking blankly out his dark window. Behind him, on both sides of the aisle were numerous couples in lively conversation, too young to care about their own sleep or those resting nearby. Their chatter gave way to the clicking data-entry keyboard of a young go-getter in a business suit. Susan mused, "Probably on Kwajalein to sell the government some over-priced commodity or service." She held her hands out behind the old woman ahead of her in a caring gesture.

Beyond the man with the lap-top computer were two older folks on either side of the aisle. She thought the woman's large hairdo looked totally inappropriate on a person obviously along in years and the rouge and "pancake" makeup encouraged the woman's indistinguishable features to appear orange and wrinkled. "Ghastly," Susan thought as she turned to the opposite side of the aisle and saw the old man. Her thoughts screamed a quite exclamation.

"Ohmigod, it's gotta be him!"

Something in her mind smothered a sudden reaction, knowing that throwing out indications of alarm upon her face could be disastrous. As if to punctuate her profound misgivings, the man ducked a bit behind his newspaper and further raised her cautions. She felt her eyes become slits of suspicion, "Yes, those eyebrows, that hair, they've gotta be fake! It's him!"

Susan stared at the "old man" a long moment then suddenly snapped herself back to reality. She continued to offer help to the elderly woman and moved thankfully out of the old man's line of vision. In her mind she reviewed the height, weight and other physical characteristics of Rear Admiral Jessup concluding that she had indeed picked the right person. "Of course he'd be in disguise," she judged. "He's smarter and bolder than I gave him credit for!"

In her slow walk to the rest rooms she continued to look at the passengers, but found that beyond the man she thought was Jessup, the only remaining people were mostly service men. They rested and talked low in the muted light of the plane's interior. In fact, the only people from that point back were those employed by Uncle Sam, all hoping to have some distractive fun in some place other than a mid-Pacific atoll where a person could absorb just so much of salt air and surf. In typical fashion they lolled about and spoke in quiet tones.

Naoki shunted left in his seat staying low to sneak a glance backward down the aisle at Susan. While she was still behind the little old lady with a helpful arm extended, he smiled and felt his opinion of her rise even more. As tense as she was, she found a moment to help an old woman who moved very slowly in the winter of life. The islander continued to fight his feelings of love for her because he knew she would just stay in the U.S. once she got there, probably never to see him again. He could only sigh and fall back into his seat to think.

Paul and Mark were sneaking glances around the aircraft also. Between the seatback and window Mark whispered, "Paul, I'm going forward as if to stretch my legs. I'll take a look at everyone in front of us. Then I'm going to the back."

Paul understood. "Check."

Neither Naoki or Paul had a clear idea of what Jessup looked like. Their impressions were formed from a thumbnail description Mark gave when they were all pitching about on the <u>Naoki I</u> returning from the evil island of Catena. Paul hoped in a way that Jessup was not on this aircraft. Naoki remained contemplative in his thoughts of Susan.

After many minutes, Mark returned from his trip to the front of the aircraft and headed past his two seated companions as if to use a rest room. He shot a glance at Paul and continued to walk.

*Attack of the Koto Maru*

He too, studied the passengers as he walked to the rear, eventually meeting up with Susan at the grouping of rest room compartments.

"Did you notice a certain bearded man with bushy eyebrows?" she said to Mark in hushed syllables.

"Yep, looks like it might be someone I know."

They looked at each other for validation and it gave them both pause. Susan reviewed a Latin phrase from high school she thought she'd forgot: Carpe Diem, seize the moment. It appeared they would have to do just that. It was good to know that Mark concurred with her choice of just who Jessup was.

"Those eyebrows got my attention," she said in a whisper.

"I'll say. He goofed. He should have made them look more real." Mark escorted Susan back toward their seats and also whispered. "In a way, I'm relieved. We won't have to go slinking around Schiphol Airport. Instead of Amsterdam, we've got him right here!"

The four friends talked it over then resumed their restless repose hoping Jessup didn't have a firearm or such.

The long hours that followed on the aircraft were jittery for them though they would sleep despite their apprehension. What could Jessup do at this moment? It seemed to be a better choice to wait until they arrived in Tokyo to confront him. Mark's mind worked overtime. He didn't want any of the plane's passengers to be hurt if a fight should start. Eventually, he drifted off into tortured rest and shared the same imagined scenes the others were thinking.

Towards morning in the descending airplane, passengers were awakening from their snoozing, stretching and yawning into consciousness hoping the coffee would be served shortly. Some of the outer islands of Japan were coming into view in the very early morning and looked like a ragged patchwork of sewing material. From this height, the water was a mixture of blue and black shine with undetectable motion. The sky had become a fusion of blues and reds at the eastern terminator well behind the air taxi and showed signs of resulting in a perfect day below. The stratosphere prepared itself for the first glimmer of strong light above the clouds where daylight comes as rapidly as sunset.

Mark's plan was simple. He reviewed it in his mind and tried to quell his knotted stomach. Now that they knew who the target was, they would wait on the plane in Tokyo until everyone terminating their journey got off. This would get as many people out of the way as possible despite the large number heading on to Europe.

Then they would gather at Jessup's seat and tell him the jig was up, perhaps sending Susan up front to alert the captain. After realizing that he was outnumbered four-to-one it was assumed he'd give up. It had been decided among the four comrades that Paul and Mark would be the two in charge of subduing Jessup if he made some unwanted move. Naoki would linger back near the rest rooms in order to come up from the rear, Susan would stay forward in the aircraft for her safety and Mark and Paul would be nearest the "old man with the beard", i.e. Rear Admiral Jessup. Susan had already made up her mind to try to explain things quickly to the pilot. Like blind innocents who couldn't have known, the stage was set for a scene of deadly possibility and freakish surprise.

Meanwhile aboard the Koto Maru, Captain Matsumoto peered through his field glasses at the bridge of the captive ship riding alongside him in parallel course. The ships were making good time now heading eventually for Tokyo as the sun began to perform its usual morning displays.

Though he could see the freighter easily in the early light he had wished to keep extra distance between the two ships at night. During the dark hours he held them apart by one mile of open water. Weather predictions were received and calm seas were expected. Below-normal wind velocities would prevail. It made the captain suppose it was the best day he had ever sailed in his long life, both now and in times before. The good captain was grateful for calm weather, for with all his skills, he knew he was a little rusty, and who needs bad weather?

Ranar was left to simmer in the brig on the KOTO along with the other organizers of the questionable voyage.

"You'll be tried in Brussels, you know."

Ranar had heard the admiral's words earlier and just looked away.

"What made you think of such deadly dealings - you, a sultan's son?"

"I do not have to explain my motives to someone as stupid as you!"

The admiral put it as succinctly as he could. "Stupid? I'm not the one on the wrong side of these bars."

At the last minute, Admiral Ingram had decided to ride on the bridge of the container ship mainly because he'd never done it. He also thought it would be easier to get off at Tokyo while all the attention was focused on the Koto. He also wanted to taunt the hell out of someone he perceived as an arrogant spoiled brat.

"You're exactly the kind of misfit we're going to be discussing at my conference in Tokyo. You'll be a damn good example, and you'll help me get my point across." The admiral noted the disgust on Ranar's face and turned on his heel to leave. "Thank you so very much!"

Ningo had taken some of his young Timano sailors to be with Admiral Ingram on the freighter to maintain sensible control of the wayward crew, even if they had already capitulated. When the ship neared port Ningo didn't want anyone jumping off with escape in mind. Though the islanders had baby-faces, there was also a look of ferocity in their collective countenance. As the ships sped away from the encroaching dawn, the crew of the captured freighter remained docile, resigning themselves to the outcome of their wicked ways. None of them wanted to be in front of the Koto's guns ever again. On the battleship, Tony continued to steer a perfect course for Captain Matsumoto.

News agencies in Japan and around the world were beginning to keep pace with events as they happened regarding the old ship. Enterprising reporters from anywhere in the immediate area hopped on planes and choppers in hopes of being the one who sent back the first pictures of the Japanese battlewagon, a sight not seen nor ever expected to be seen by modern man so many years after it was launched. The two ships were about two days out of port providing adequate time to whip the general populace into a frenzy of patriotic feelings. The news media licked its chops at the sensation about to come steaming into Tokyo Bay nearly fifty years and two sizeable wars late to the quay. A squadron of choppers left Tokyo to try for the first picture.

Fortunately, the Japanese media were unaware of the other drama which would be landing on their shores in a much shorter time. Flight 712 from Kwajalein atoll could be seen from the ground as a spotlight in the fading dark of night on its final approach to Tokyo. The vibrating light looked like something akin to a UFO hanging in the air seeming not to move, coming in slowly over Tokyo Bay to land at the old international airport. Some flights still came in at the outdated airport and were mostly from military outposts. The activity was at times, brisk.

Aboard the flight, a few passengers readied themselves for debarking at Tokyo but about half were staying on until Amsterdam. Morning light fell across the man with the bushy eyebrows who sank once again behind his newspaper. He read the tabloid nervously just as the wheels slammed to the concrete runway under him. The wheels spun with no choice of their own in the mad torture of trying to support a speeding jetliner. Shock absorbers collapsed inward and upward with an extended hiss. The metal of struts and beams torqued and tested their temper in the maze of carefully engineered landing gear. The craft was down safely on all threes. Mark noticed Jessup make no preparation to get off at Tokyo.

A few interminable minutes after landing, the Airbus approached the terminal area whining its engines lower and lower until finally reaching idle and coming to a stop. Apprehension knotted the stomaches of four good friends as they

*Attack of the Koto Maru*

realized "show time" was here. Each one felt enormous responsibility for the safety of others on the airplane.

The craft was parked out about five hundred feet from the airport buildings near two ferry buses with drivers waiting patiently, arms folded. Only one vehicle would be needed for the few debarking passengers, but both drivers remained outside their buses to assist the sleepy travelers. Those who were just now streaming out of the cabin spouted impatient chatter and headed down the staircase to the waiting buses.

On the plane, the exiting passengers continued to walk past Mark and Paul except the woman with the huge hairdo, who was obviously getting off at Tokyo but having quite a time gathering herself together. It made the wait difficult for the two men ready to spring into action. The two of them waited for the woman to pass by with knots, almost pains in their stomachs. They noticed Naoki at the back who was also charged-up and ready.

When the beefy woman finally passed by them, Mark and Paul got to their feet with careful motions and walked toward the bearded man. The man noticed their unusual stare and the cat-like way they approached him. When he sat up and looked back at Naoki advancing from the rear he slowly came to his feet, eyes enlarging.

"Okay, Jessup! Give it up!"

All the men jumped toward the man with the beard and began subduing his panicked movements. He got in one good hit across Naoki's head and continued to escalate the fray. The woman with all the hair was at the door and Susan had to look through the big hairdo to see the altercation.

The pilots and service people were also trying to get a look past the ball of hair when it unexpectedly caught on a section of the door opening. The snagged hair jerked weirdly backwards and peeled completely off the woman exposing Susan to a face to face encounter with Admiral Jessup!

"Aiiggh!" Susan screamed with astonished fright.

Paul looked to the front of the aircraft just as Naoki gave a mighty tug on the old man's beard. The bewildered man yelled with a Jewish accent, "Vot you Vant! I got no money."

Admiral Jessup, in half-drag minus his bouffant wig pushed Susan into the crew and smacked a steward with a lead blackjack. He clawed desperately down the staircase pushing and stomping anyone in his way, hitting and slamming even women as he went. Susan yelled, "C'mon guys, he's here!"

Susan began forcing her way along through the gatherings of people down the staircase to the waiting buses. A driver tried to stop Jessup and learned swiftly about the knockout power of the old leaden blackjacks. Jessup hit the driver hard enough to knock him out where he stood and dashed up into the driver's seat of the vacant second bus. The men in Susan's group appeared at the top of the stairs and watched the tenacious woman push her way through the crowd toward the bus.

"Susan, don't...!" Paul shouted.

The brave woman reached the back end of the bus as Jessup found the gear he needed to get the thing in motion.

"Oh, nooo!"

The omnibus jerked a couple times and tore off dragging a clinging Susan who had managed to grasp a service ladder on the back of the vehicle. She ran along in bounding stride holding on to the ladder until a breathless crowd watched her make her way onto the vehicle and disappear with it around a parked aircraft. Immediately she grabbed the London police whistle from her wrist and blew it wildly. When the absurdity of it hit her, she tossed the noisemaker sideways.

It was some time before the airport police could react and it was going to be even longer until Mark could fully explain what happened. Eventually, and after many precious minutes ticked off, the police, along with Mark, Paul and Naoki charged forward in pursuit of the purloined empty bus with Susan Black riding the exterior. Jessup was running all around the airport looking for a way out, searching his memory regarding the terrain and what was located where.

On the speeding bus, the Cincinnatian climbed higher on the ladder until she rounded the rooftop. Soon on top, the speed of the bus didn't seem quite as fast to her as when she was clinging to the ladder down near the swiftly passing concrete. She had a good overview of where Jessup was going and what his options were. It was a bit easier to hold on laying flat on top.

"Why am I here?" she enunciated to nobody.

Jessup, on the other hand was in a frenzied panic, trying to remember where the golf course and marina were located. "Somewhere near the airport's eastern perimeter fence," he thought.

The madman raced down a taxiway upsetting the air controller's delicate balance of arriving and departing flights and causing more trouble than he was ready to cope with. In a moment, he realized it was not a place for ground vehicles and opted to speed off on a side runway. "It's down this way, I know it is!"

Susan laid flat facing forward on a ladder which ran the length of the bus top. She supposed it might be used for luggage but it was empty except for a sizeable tool box tied at the extreme front. Seeing the box slam and bang on the roof gave her an idea.

Jessup turned many corners on the airport's gigantic concrete streets with no obvious escape route discernable. In the speeding bus he screeched a right hand turn directly into the path of a light aircraft taking off. The pilot pulled quickly on the joystick and stopped breathing as the bus zipped under him. Even though he'd made it over the bus safely, he fought to regain control from the unexpected confrontation rediscovering at the same time why men in responsible positions always use deodorant. Diapers wouldn't have been a bad idea either. He and the copilot leveled the plane in its climb and wordlessly examined one another's moist foreheads.

The desperate Jessup was driving faster and more erratically ploughing left and then right heading south on the main runway.

Susan, holding on for dear life was sliding left, then right, then left again unable to look where the maniacal Jessup was going.

When the bus seemed to be going straight ahead, she finally looked up and judged their location to be about midway down a main runway. A new noise began to buffet her eardrums, a shaking whine that seemed all around grinding its way into her head, through her skull and into her very bones. She took a quick look over her shoulder and let out a scream which may have been heard downtown.

"Aaiigh!"

Directly behind her with engines screaming was the nose of a 747 tilting up in takeoff mode. She knew in her heart it would not miss the bus. Jessup saw it in the rear-view mirror and put the pedal down. There just wasn't enough moxie in the service vehicle to move it any faster. All he had was hope.

The copilot of the giant jet promptly spit his coffee between his legs and into the cushion. The copilot dropped his cup on the floor. Both men knew there wasn't enough time or distance to abort the takeoff. All they could do was quickly snap up the nose wheels, continue with takeoff protocol and hope the people beneath them survived. They figured it was a plus to have the runway intruders located under the middle of the plane, not in the path of the main wheels.

The rising monster's nose wheels quickly caught up with the ground transporter coming to within what the prone woman thought must have been millimeters of her backbone. The underbelly of the giant slid along just inches above her head which she kept low imprinting the bus with her face. "It's the end!" she cried feeling the nose wheels snag some of her hair on the way past.

The jet's main wheels straddled the bus for what seemed like an hour of slow-motion. A silent, shocked Susan tried to think but couldn't hear her own scream, watching the violent rotation of the wheels pass by her face vibrating within their shock absorbing mechanisms. Without knowing why, she shouted,

*Attack of the Koto Maru*

"Mom and dad would never believe this! Jesus Christ protect me!"

She pressed one ear to the bus top and held her free hand hard against the other. The roar of the engines still took her eardrums to a point where they could only register a dull thud when they passed from behind her to ahead of her. It was sensory overload from hell, not counting the rest of the scenario. She considered herself lucky to be between the blasting engines, not directly behind.

The aircraft's monstrous sheetmetal finally lifted away from the bus and thundered off into the waiting blue heavens. It left Susan to wonder if she had actually relieved herself or just felt a little extra warmth in her karma area. Black backwash from the jet engines blew her around on the roof like a wind sock on a post at the exact moment she regripped the rails with her free hand. Carbon specks from the jet engines peppered her hands painfully as her throbbing brain issued a gritty reminder of things not to do on a vacation. "I'm glad there's no tail engine," she said with great relief feeling the battering and the spray of carbon particles subside. She composed herself immediately into the other emergency at hand, thankful to be alive and swearing to the heavens she would be attending church as soon as possible.

The frantic driver brought the vehicle to the end of the main runway and as expected was able to see a golf course and marina through the trees. He suddenly turned off the concrete and over the dusty apron heading directly for the twenty-foot fence about five hundred yards away. He sensed someone's presence on the roof and shot off some nine-millimeter handgun rounds. The uneven surface under him caused him to shoot wildly, never touching Susan who saw the slugs come ripping up through the roof. "How much worse can this get?" she asked herself in staccato rhythms. "Ohh, Lorrrdd, protect me one last time!"

She bounced to and fro over the uneven ground surface nearly frightened to death but again managed to regain herself. Just before the aircraft passed overhead, the clinging woman had slithered forward to the tool chest and noticed it was tied loosely with one long strap.  She marveled that it hadn't fallen off yet then hurriedly pulled it backward along the luggage rail to the limit of the elastic strap.  When the bouncing bus stopped its severest motion for a moment she pushed the tool box forward with every bit of strength she had.  Between her and the rubber band, the box sprang straight off the leading edge of the roof and way beyond the length of the well-stretched strap.

Jessup watched the heavy tool box go straight out into the air to the overstretched limit of its tether and twang back with a vengeance through the glass of his windshield.

After the smash occurred, Susan knew she'd struck paydirt.  The bus immediately began to pitch and veer wickedly as Jessup's anger became that of a wildcat.  I'll kill whoever you are!" he yelled shooting off rounds with abandon.  Through the blood and glass he was still able to see the golf course ahead.  He aimed the bus at the tall fence and threw his spent gun on the floor.

Susan saw what he was intending and eased her grip on the rack.  She slid quickly to the extreme back of the bus roof freezing her grip on the rack once again and bracing herself for fence debris.

"Oh, Lordy!"

Jessup had his bus going about fifty mph when he neared the fence but he failed to see the deep drainage ditch just before the mesh.  The front wheels went slamming into the gutter, then out, then onward through the fence.  If Susan had any hope of holding on it was lost forever when the rear wheels hit the ditch.

The resulting bump from the back wheels going in and out of the trench magnified itself through the coil springs and threw Susan high in the air over fence and tree top, handing her over to good luck, the good Lord, and fortunate happenstance.  An end-over-end flight brought the lucky woman safely down through some small tree tops and onto a tarpaulin which covered a large compost pile.  She landed with a softness she didn't quite believe.  After the unexpected cloud-like landing she said,

"Some days it just works!" After that, collapsing into repose was inevitable. She lay still a moment and caught her breath.

"I wonder where the others are?" she panted.

The formerly flying female glanced down and away from her feathery landing to see Jessup in his stolen bus go tearing across golf greens and fairways like some mad stunt driver purposely trying to cause mischief. After he went out of sight beyond some trees she figured he'd made it to the water's edge about half a mile away. There were boats galore over there and God knows he probably found one to use for getting away.

Still a little dazed but glad to be at a standstill, she collapsed again and rested a moment. In the distance she heard a hoard of official cars heading toward the gaping hole in the runway fence. She murmured a prayerful benediction to the whole mess then counted her arms and legs again. Jessup's path across the golf course would be easy to track for it left an ugly scar. The numbers of duffers who had managed to jump out of the way would be witness enough. She flopped back and rested for another delectable moment in the warm sun, her chest still heaving.

The airport cars skidded and pulled up to her location spewing their human contents into the morning sun. Officials of all kinds were soon on the scene and at first did not see Susan still high atop the compost pile.

"Hey! Hey, you guys!" she shouted from her vantage point.

Naoki quickly went to her aid with rounded eyes that could be seen a block away. Paul yelled, "How the hell did you get up there?"

"You might be hard put to believe it!"

The police got two of their cars past the fence debris and careened across the golfing area, further damaging the club's prideful greenery. Susan slid down the tarp into the waiting and very willing arms of the rugged Timanoan who always seemed to be first at her side. He wrapped a massive hug around her and said, "I didn't think you'd live through it!"

When they broke apart, Naoki was embarrassed with the tears in his eyes, prompting Susan to parade herself to show she was okay. "See, merchandise still undamaged." Her laugh cancelled his deep concern and he laughed haltingly with her.

"Uh, oh. I know somebody who's going to be mad as a hornet," Paul said as he opened the suitcase of cash he found nearby.

"That's great! It doesn't matter as much now if he gets away. The main thing is we got his payoff money! The police will get him before long anyway."

Susan entered in with sarcasm, "Yes, three million will go a long way toward alleviating our national debt. Har har."

Naoki said, "The police don't seem to be in a big hurry either. If he made it to the marina and stole a boat he's still in Tokyo harbor and it's just a matter of time until he's located. But..."

"But, what?" Susan wondered.

"Well, I don't think it's good to have him that angry."

*Attack of the Koto Maru*

# CHAPTER EIGHTEEN

In the glitzy city of Tokyo, Japan, ancient legends of the Shinto gods and displays of Buddhist trappings take a back seat to mega-traffic jams and people rushing to fill any spot recently vacated by another. It is a city on the move, adding new workers daily to the beehive atmosphere of a town expanding its activity wildly in two-digit multipliers. Nothing stands still in Tokyo but the buildings, and even they sway once in a while.

But if a city could be compared to wrist watches, Tokyo would have the Swiss movement. Commuters run or walk fast all the time being loathe to miss their proper train or other conveyance. Business hums at a swift clip, computers run nonstop and businessmen drink far too much after hours. If the train system breaks down, Tokyo enjoys the same chaos its counterpart in the U.S. does - near collapse until repairs are made. Everyone who draws breath in this metropolis has been stranded a time or two.

Despite doomsayers who say that anything moving so fast must one day crash and burn, this "busiest city in the world" shows no sign of letting up. And too, in the face of experts who say Japan will one day sink into the sea in a giant tsunami or earthquake, the city just goes on building and building toward some frenzied conclusion. Growth is postulated aplenty by master planners who will likely never see the Asian metropolis in its finished state. All who come here are smitten by the speed of the city and the kind hospitality of the Japanese. It's difficult to impede the pace of a city like this for even a minute, but a fifty-year-old mystery battleship steaming into port might do the job nicely.

"Wow," Susan remarked, watching from the monorail window. "It's not as high as I thought."

None of the four friends had ever been on a monorail, but gliding on its smooth single rail remains the best way to get downtown from the old airport area. Naoki likened it to

*Alan De Wolfe*

Superman's view of the city and Paul marveled at the engineering. Mark was just happy the whole adventure seemed to come to a good resolution considering everything that could have gone wrong. The <u>Koto Maru</u> was a day and a half out of port, scheduled to arrive Thursday morning in full dress with many private boats saluting her. Expectations were running high. The adventurers planned to view the arrival from the best place possible, aboard one of the harbor tugs. The city was getting ready to party.

"Look at this!" Paul said, pointing at a headline in the morning edition of Japan's largest newspaper.

<u>"Mystery battleship heading for Tokyo"</u>

Mark said, "Let's get over to the embassy and find out where she'll be tied up. This is one party I don't wanna miss. We can go sightseeing this afternoon. Don't forget. We're keeping an eye open for you know who."

Exiting the downtown terminal the group taxied its way to the U.S. Embassy located across the street from a collection of buildings comprising the Kyodo News Service. As might be expected, their visit was cut short. They were quickly asked to cross the street and meet with newsmen for an in-depth story of the coming battlewagon. Naoki Matsumoto, soon to be hailed as one of the great shoppers of the world tried to beg-off but the clambering newsmen would not have it. A mad scene immediately surrounded the group who were quickly blinded by photographers and examined scrupulously by writers. In the giant hubbub created by their presence, reporters tried to glean from them even the smallest detail of their gripping tale of the sea.

With all the derring-do of their exploits, and with special emphasis on their heroism, Susan, Mark, Naoki and Paul were having their lives changed drastically by the print of newspapers and the sound bites of television. After the afternoon's extra editions and the six o'clock news, their anonymity would be lost forever. How could Jessup possibly miss all this?

Naoki said, "This is hard to believe!"

*Attack of the Koto Maru*

"Wait till the ship comes in!" Paul referenced.

All four of them would find themselves described in detail as international champions in the morning editions of Tokyo tabloids. With pictures and headlines splashed around the world, their fame was bound to grow fast in a world hungry for heros. Susan's ride atop the bus would certainly be a hit, a thing she couldn't have envisioned four weeks ago. The tsunami, the attack of the Koto Maru on an island run by a despot, the involvement of an American admiral - it was all here. Even fiction couldn't top it.

A picture of Jessup had been found in some archive and it too was scheduled to hit the press. Fishermen and dock workers all along the waterfront were sending in wild stories of the admiral dressed in half-drag running here and there shocking the pants off bewildered sailors. The angry, frustrated ex-admiral knew his way around Tokyo Bay which tipped authorities that he wouldn't be an easy catch. However, Mark felt that due to the thoroughness of the Japanese police, capture was inevitable. In his run, the fugitive would barely have time to stop and change out of his female clothing.

Right now, while they were still relatively unknown, Mark, Naoki, Susan and Paul wanted to get hold of some clothes that fit better than the ones from Kwajalein. The embassy had secured rooms for them nearby in the Mandarin Princess Hotel and the female member of the entourage wanted very much to shower. "How many visitors end up on a compost pile," she wondered with a smile. Mark was happy she was in one piece. "It wasn't too bad. Suppose there had been no tarp!"

"Hmmm. That is a point."

Thanks to the newspapers, tomorrow morning all of Tokyo would be anticipating the Koto's Thursday docking near the Hama Rikyu Garden not far from the Asahi Shimbun offices. It was a nice central location and would provide maximum visual impact for displaying a type of ship not seen here in several decades. The Japanese press was eating it up, preparing to amaze the population with even more outrageous headlines. Mark continued to wonder about Jessup.

Once the two ships arrived, the captive freighter carrying Admiral Ingram would be docked somewhat further away near the Takeshiba Pier so that authorities could seal it off until U.S. personnel arrived to accompany the Japanese bomb squads. There was no hurry once the old container freighter was secured. Tokyo settled into its daily routine with great anticipation.

"Where the heck is Jessup," Mark said to Paul.

"I can imagine he's a slippery devil. Didn't he used to be stationed here?"

"Yeah, he's gotta have some friends or at least he knows where to go to hide. I'm not leaving here until he's found."

"I'll stick around too. We've seen it this far along, let's see it ended."

"This is a heck of a town," Susan quipped.

Naoki added, "Yes, I want to see it all!"

The islander's comment dictated the events of the next two days. They all longed for a little city life and took in all the sights of Tokyo and vicinity. Naoki got box after box of freshly shopped clothes ready for transport to Timano. He planned to sell them or give them away to the friends who could not be here with him. Paul and Mark kept a sharp lookout for Jessup but to no immediate avail. Susan enjoyed a perfect secretary's vacation and all the popularity she could handle. Everyone had fun and everyone wondered about the evil admiral.

When at last the days and hours wound down to Thursday morning, teeming multitudes began to collect at every available shore position along the Tokyo waterfront growing to at least eight deep everywhere in sight. That figure changed by the minute with uncountable heads of straight shiny hair shimmering in long waves of black. All eyes looked out to sea for the native ship lost to them for so long. Enterprising merchants sold hasty renditions of <u>Yamato</u>-class battlewagon photos to excited throngs who couldn't get enough. A few lucky photographers got pictures of the <u>Koto Maru</u> at sea and sold them to the

*Attack of the Koto Maru*

newspapers. Naoki was amazed to see the ship emblazoned in feature after feature, always pictured riding next to its captive ship. One picture showed his father smiling hugely from the bridge. Despite the fact that it nearly made him cry, he cut the picture out and stashed it among the boxes of clothing. They'd all had a difficult time the last few days. Now it was time for celebration.

Mark and his special companions found their way to the tug which would carry them out to view the Koto up close for she was due to enter the outer harbor any minute. The Nimitz was finally fixed and would be about a half day behind. Paul's thoughts drifted out over the bright green sea to his tiny sloop still safe in the carrier's big seawell. In his mind he reckoned the whole thing had been quite an adventure, but he was glad to see it finished.

The captain of the tug yelled some loud Japanese words and the lines were cast off. The tough little boat floated out from its dock, came around to face southeast and putted its way clear of other vessels.

The engines droned faster and hummed deeper as the boat's complement let its collective anticipation grow. This was it, the moment Naoki and the other young men of Timano had wanted for so long. Finally, on a crystal-clear day in a time-warp if ever there was one, their dreams were being realized. From the deck of the tug he heard the Koto Maru sound its distant horn. A roar went out from the crowd, the celebration was beginning.

A lot has been written on the pages of time, whether in ancient prose or modern history books about the awesome stature and menacing nature of fighting ships. But on this day, for the Japanese standing in the crowd nothing ever written could equal the dark silhouette on the horizon of Tokyo Bay. A Yamato-class battleship was almost as terrible seen at a distance as up close. This generation of Japanese could not conceive of any sight as awesome. Most people viewing the approaching behemoth fell quiet to pursue their own imaginings.

*Alan De Wolfe*

Without warning, Captain Matsumoto discharged dummy rounds from two of the biggest forward guns. They had been prepared earlier on Timano for just such an occasion and they wowed Admiral Ingram, watching from the container ship. He wanted all of Tokyo to hear the blast of guns likely never to be fired again. He hoped it would stir an even greater interest in his conference. The two cannons were almost vertical showing a huge puff of smoke before the actual detonation was heard by those on shore. The thud was like none ever heard by this generation and brought an enthusiastic roar from the dazzled crowd. People aboard the yachts and other private boats riding alongside the Koto were shocked at the power of this "Made in Japan" beauty. Tokyo Bay never had such a moment. It was from a ship originally meant to menace the rest of the civilized world. Admiral Ingram could only stare with pride.

Plowing steadily forward the Koto loomed bigger and bigger, like the inexorable advance of a comet or the sinister approach of a beast in a spicy-food nightmare. Captain Matsumoto purposely had his ship precede the freighter into the harbor so that nothing would mar the total visual experience. The young men aboard had made sure the pennants and streamers were run up in great profusion and strung perfectly from mast tip to the ship's ends. The battlewagon not only looked new, the colorful blaze of streamers enhanced its appearance and left no doubt.

The harbor pilot had boarded the Koto at the entrance to the bay long before the crowd could see the ship and was dazzled beyond comprehension. He'd never ushered a battlewagon like this into the tricky harbor and was very nervous. He relied very much on Captain Matsumoto's good instincts, then gave the order to gently nudge the engines. The crew brought the big boy further into the harbor with all due caution.

The freighter began to descend in speed behind the Koto and trail off slowly to its appointed pier. Admiral Ingram again felt an odd twinge of satisfaction watching the battleship ahead of him maneuver into a harbor it would everlastingly call home. It brought a tear to his eye. Would anyone be in the hotel meeting rooms to begin the disarmament conference? Would they all be here instead? He still hoped to get the conference held aboard the Koto and silently wished he'd stayed on the battleship after they'd waylaid the container ship.

Captain Matsumoto watched with enormous pride as a cheer went up from the shore-bound crowds. His heart nearly burst with sentiment as the Koto's engines were tenderly and easily brought to an undulating stop in front of so many people. The Koto Maru let off two last vertical explosions from the forward guns stunning the crowd, then fell silent forever. Massive fireworks erupted over the ship just as the resonance from the guns fell off. It totally surprised the crew and everyone else but added to the anticipation. Now the tugs would do their bumping and pushing to get the massive ship docked properly.

Naoki and friends were on the tug nearest the wheelhouse of the Koto. From far below, he looked up to the flying bridge and saw his father more proud and close to tears than he had ever thought possible. His own tears drizzled out of his prideful eyes when his father gave him a long look acknowledging him with a salute. Tony popped out to display a smile that seemed to light up the ship.

"We made it!" he yelled to Naoki.

Naoki was nearly overcome until he noticed Susan bawling like a child. His only thought was to wrap an arm around her. Her emotions cancelled his own sentimentality and he went hastily to her side.

The mass of the ship's bulk continued to cause a roar of approval from the mad crowd even above the sound of the tugs. Captain Matsumoto and a few of his old mariners finally had what they always wanted - to be welcomed home as heroes and to be cheered by raving countrymen. When the gangplank was lowered at the makeshift docking pier they, and all the excited young crew stepped out to walk down into the adoring swarm, waving and shouting in a furious clamor.

*Alan De Wolfe*

Unbeknownst to the old sailors, the press had gone way back into the newspaper archives and dug up the hometown stories of their first journeys out to sea. In the next editions, the old men would find out more about themselves than they could remember. Naoki was quick to luxuriate in his father's embrace when they met at the lower end of the gangplank.

"Well done, father!" he shouted into the captain's ear.

"Thank you, son," was the only thing Naoki heard as the multitudes swept his smiling, weeping father off into their squeeze. It was a festive moment for all aboard the <u>Koto Maru</u> and for all on shore. The crew of the ship along with Mark, Paul, Naoki and Susan were nudged along to waiting limousines for an International Trade Center reception. It was a day never to be forgot. Everyone in the throng was joyfully drunk with emotion and happy to remain standing in the shadow of the monstrously quiet ship. The citizens of the big city filed by to touch the ships ropes.

In a gathering as auspicious as this, it's easy to spot the exceptional person who through it all remains serious. Most people are caught with small smiles or big grins on their faces when the occasion is a happy one. In its revelry, this Tokyo Bay crowd tended to overlook the humorless expression pinched up under a disguising stick-on beard displayed by the sour face of an ex-rear admiral whose only reason to live was revenge. Though he stood in the crowd, Jessup did not admire the <u>Koto Maru</u>. He had his eyes on the freighter docked about a quarter mile away. Misery was in his heart and a large portion of revenge filled his mind.

Not much later in a city still humming with revelry, evening breezes arrived delicately off the water and stirred warm salty air along the waterfront scene. Floodlights illuminated the <u>Koto</u> off in the distance and Mark, who had left the party mostly to escape it, observed the old ship easily from the other dock - the one accommodating Ranar's freighter. He continued to lean on his elbows at the dock rail and contemplated the breezy ambiance of the dimly lit waterfront. It was a sweet night, full of love and

*Attack of the Koto Maru*

good will. Lights twinkled in the city's skyline behind the distant battleship, walkers continued to stand beneath it still awed by its very presence, throngs milled around its quay and probably would until morning. The ship was home at last. It was quite a sight even from a distance.

Mark walked alongside the freighter in a contemplative milieu. The soiree celebrating this event was typically excessive even for the Japanese, and he surmised they didn't yet realize all the fun they would have with the old battleship in the next few months. The gala at the trade center was to continue well into the night. He was glad to be here in the night's comparative quiet with some easy thoughts.

In the steamy, smokey smell of mists trailing around the dock's greasy unloading fixtures, he mellowed out until ripe and let his eyes trace the deck area above on the old freighter. A guard walked here and there on the decks but everything was mostly low-key. The old freighter lent its soft lighting to the mixture of thoughts and memories wafting off the feathery wrinkles of his mind.

He imagined Paul would have his little boat back and probably would return to exactly what he was doing when all this hit the fan, Naoki would shop till he dropped again tomorrow and then probably go to the U.S. and enroll in some university. Mark himself would go back to a hero's welcome at the Pentagon and probably get some incredible commission, and Susan...

He heard a car door shut behind him and turned to see Susan exiting a limo

"Hi," she said, walking up to him.

"Hi," he returned. "I was just thinking about you and what you might do when your life gets back to normal."

Susan sighed, "I've been giving it a lot of thought too. These last few days will make my job with the defense department ultra-boring. It's been good to see places other than the good old U.S.A. and to realize those places are nice too."

"Yes. After a paradise like Timano or the other islands, the big culture shock is what you find when you get home."

"I'll say!"

Both friends sensed a need for quiet after the events on the sea and the mad confusion of the party fun.

"I lost Paul, but Naoki's still at the ball living it up."

"Oh?" Mark said, still leaning on the rail. The willowy woman from Cincinnati leaned also. "Yes. I'm reasonably sure the guy's never had so much attention."

"He can party all right! One can tell from that devilish glint in his eye."

Susan paused, changed her look and continued.

"Mark, I want to thank you for all you did to keep me safe. I've had more good luck in the last few days than anyone should have in a lifetime."

He tried to diffuse her seriousness. "At least now you know what the top of those airport buses look like," he laughed. "You're a heck of a gal!"

Susan had come looking for him to tell him something important and would not be denied.

"I'm going to marry Naoki."

"What?"

Her sudden invective shocked Mark. He wasn't quite prepared for her words. His own abiding postulations regarding marriage to Susan were, too quickly, nothing but dust. To remain a true gentleman he would have to snap himself into the present reality and ready himself to show support. Susan went on.

"Yes, he asked me again just before the party, this time he was quite earnest. I love all you guys but didn't think I was ready to give my heart. After seeing life as it is on his island and the warm simplicity of his nature, I began to realize it's everything I've been looking for. Although he wants to go to the U.S. for awhile, he also wants to call Timano home and that sounds so good to me. I have no honest reason for liking Washington or remaining in its sooted atmosphere."

"I'm sure you'll be happy," Mark mustered. "Naoki is a good man and an honest guy."

Laughing she said, "You should have seen the way his jaw hit the floor when I said yes."

"I'll bet!" he agreed. "I'm a little shocked myself but I'm very happy for you." He enfolded her with his arms feeling some disappointment yet wanting the best for her. It was his last big hug of a dream that might have been. Engaged as they were in the last emotion of their flickering attraction, neither one of them noticed a dark figure advance from a nearby shadow. Fortunately it was friendly.

"And I thought I had the inside track," Paul lamented with a chortle. The three of them looked at one another and instantly experienced total understanding. They laughed and hugged at the same time. Paul had surprised them deliciously as he liked to do by stepping out from a dark area. He was also happy for Susan and let her know with a kiss to the cheek.

"You've got yourself a good man, girlie." Their adventure was over, but it was obvious to each they would always be the best of friends.

"If I go back to beachcombing in the islands, I'll see you and Naoki all the time. And Mark will have to visit as often as possible. It'll be fun! But no more tsunamis please!"

"You've got to write your book!" she asserted.

"Oh, maybe. Sounds like work to me, and you know how I feel about that!"

Each was feeling on top of the world during the next big group hug. Mark absentmindedly looked beyond Susan's embrace and up at the ship's rail high above them.

He stared blankly at first then felt a dawning light wash through his brain. He froze in an attentive stance telegraphing his feelings through his body. Quietly but urgently he mouthed words into the ears of his two companions. "Keep hugging and don't look around at the ship!"

The other two obeyed instinctively having heard such urgencies before. In a moment they broke from the group embrace somewhat puzzled keeping their eyes on Mark as if in conversation. Mark continued to notice the ship's rail out the corner of his vision not believing what he thought he saw.

"It's Jessup," he said in a whisper.

Paul smiled to distract. "On the ship?"

"Yes. He's looking over the rail. Now he's walking away."

"Are you sure?"

"Not entirely, but whoever that was is wearing a phony beard, I could tell from here! And we already know what a good disguise artist he is."

Lieutenant Mark Ingram decided it was time to show his bars to the two gangplank guards. "Paul, come with me. Susan, see if you can get my father and some security forces on the phone. Tell him to get down here right away!"

The three of them bolted into action so fast that the armed guards stiffened as the men ran toward them. Susan sprinted for a pay phone wondering if she had the right coins.

"We're not supposed to let anyone on the ship...sir."

The MPs had to halt the speedy lieutenant but knew in the end they would defer to his wishes. He was, after all, instrumental in stopping the ship from accomplishing its original mission of delivering A-bombs. "Where's your superior, young man."

"In the wheelhouse, sir."

"You're gonna have to let us aboard, M.P. I'll take care of it."

"Yessir!"

"Has anyone else gone past you tonight?"

"No sir. But the waterline doors were open for awhile."

"Oh hell, that's how he got aboard, I just know it!" Alarm struck him and Paul at the same moment."

"You two wait here for the admiral but keep everyone else away."

"Yessir!"

With Paul a step behind him and the guards left to their wonderment, Mark didn't hesitate to race up the walkway and

*Attack of the Koto Maru*

head for deck two, where the unfinished bombs were located. Neither of them knew what Jessup was doing aboard nor exactly how he got there but whatever the reason, it couldn't be for the good of mankind. The alarm they felt began to heighten. Electricity sparked through their bodies, adrenaline kicked in big time.

They could see the control bridge high above them as they walked in a quiet rush toward the superstructure. Windows were alight and shadows moved against the glass panes on the bridge but there was no time to alert the few men onboard. In view of the dread both men were feeling they knew it would be better to stalk Jessup by themselves and not call for the onboard militia just yet. Caution was deeply on their minds. They could hardly believe that the danger and fear of the last few days had returned to haunt them. They stepped over the hatch entry and moved into the ship's corridor maze.

Inside, a long companionway led all the way through the superstructure in a long bend. On most container ships, the five-story control structure is located rising straight up from the stern decks with the command bridge at the very top. The high structure is purposely located at the rear so the containers can be observed constantly from the wheelhouse in case of unsafe shifting. The immense superstructure is also living quarters for the crew. Meeting rooms are located here, and also smoking rooms and activity rooms necessary to fight boredom. There were a few dim night lights in the long corridor and seemingly no guards. Ranar's men had been taken to join him in jail and the Timano Island men were at the big bash. Security was scant, almost careless.

About halfway down the corridor a pointed sliver of light illuminated the carpeting from a door ajar in the windward bulkhead of the interior. The area they were heading toward brought a reminder to them both.

"That's where the bombs are," Mark whispered.

"If I were Jessup, that's where I'd be," Paul added.

As if knowing what would be best, Paul slinked down the companionway past the lighted room devising a plan as he went. Mark understood wordlessly and sneaked to the first door, pushing it open slowly and carefully.

He swung the door inward on its well-oiled hinges with as much stealth as possible, though a tiny squeak occurred. From what he could see, the bombs were undisturbed. Emboldened and seeing no one, he stepped in and approached the cases looking at them one by one, panning the room as he walked.

In the deathly quiet, all bombs looked the same as before with the critical wiring still hanging off to the side for want of a detonator. He walked and looked and was rather surprised not to see more guards. "Humph. All at the party," he guessed.

Noiselessly he closed in on the last bomb in the row, a casing marked "number six" and expected Paul to step through the further doorway straight ahead. He drew near and peered over the edge of casing number six. It caused him a blink of recognition. Number six had a detonator partially hooked up.

<u>Crash</u>! At the very moment the detonator registered in his mind the feeling of raw steel on the back of his head gave him stars to view and a weird, full feeling in his sinuses. He instantly hit the floor and fell limp, but the blow didn't knock him out. With an actor's expertise he stifled a grimace and faked a knocked-out appearance. The voice of Admiral Jessup came through his ear holes despite the hurtful ringing. "There, you little bastard!"

Through eyes nearly closed Mark lay on the floor fully able to see the watchful Jessup return to the bomb. The detonator languished half-assembled in front of him and his nervous hands fixed and fiddled with it in a furious fidget. Mark waited for his chance to move but didn't want to be a fool about it. Jessup had his prized luger on a table within grasping range and continued his nervous glances at Mark. It was up to Paul to do something.

The lieutenant continued to lay on the floor wondering how far along Jessup was. Did he really know how to hook up an atomic bomb detonator? It certainly appeared so. What a horrific irony to have an atomic device go off here, in Japan, the only country in the world to know the aftermath before it happens. And what political chaos would come from this? It must not happen. In a queasy blur he laid on the floor putting all manner of scenes together in his mind. When his vision became clearer he knew Jessup would have to be talked out of it. He made a murmur of regaining consciousness trying not to surprise the fast-working Jessup. Hope ran through him thinking of Paul, not yet seen.

"Right there, Lieutenant!" Jessup brandished his gun.

"Admiral, nothing could be worth this," the dizzy lieutenant insisted.

Jessup, distracted from his work held his gun on Mark. He leaned against a bulkhead and yelled, "Sez you! I had it made with that three million. Now it's gone, thanks to you and your damned friends!" The fire rose up in his eyes. "Vacation, my eye! You knew all the time, didn't you!"

"No. No, I didn't. You were the farthest person from my mind. I thought that your evil bad boy from Malua was doing something, and I was getting the proof to show you. What possesses you?"

"Humph! The desire to live a little. The desire for respect I never got, thanks in part to your rotten uncle!"

Jessup put the gun aside and worked again on the detonator. "Now I'm gonna get even with everyone! In a few minutes you and me'll be hovering up about twenty-thousand feet! Only you won't be able to tell one of your molecules from another!"

"C'mon, Admiral. This accomplishes nothing."

"Ta hell it won't! My name will be in the history books - that's more than I ever got from the Pentagon!" Glaring at Mark, he picked up the luger and waved it in his face. "Everyone's gonna remember this day!"

After another long wild stare, Jessup placed the gun on the table so to bury both hands in the wiring which was becoming more complete by the minute. The luger was close enough to grab if he had to. "Just stay right where you are, Lieutenant."

Mark put his butt on a step stool, stroked the back of his head and remained far enough away for Jessup to feel comfortable. He continued to fake a dazed condition. Behind the feverishly working admiral, Mark caught a glimpse of Paul moving surreptitiously through a dark spot in the room, the tread of his foot unheard by Jessup's ears.

"There, it's about ready! All I have to do is hit that red button."

To distract Jessup from discovering Paul, Mark said, "Why should I wait over here? I mean, if I'm going to die anyway, why don't I just...jump you!" Mark yelled the last part of his statement at the same moment Paul attack the admiral.

Unfortunate for Paul, when a rather good-sized man is desperate, he is like a man possessed of demons. Jessup's strength was above normal and his instincts were strung tight and sharp. When Paul lunged at him, the admiral pulled back and Paul went beyond him. Then he came down with his fist on the side of his attacker's head knocking him to the floor and into a swirl of unglued thoughts.

By this time, Mark finally got close enough to grab Jessup's shirt. Jessup countered with a sweeping roundhouse sending his bulk a bit beyond the intended chin contact. Each man scuffled comically grasping the shirt of the other, yanking and battering themselves against the bulkheads in a dance where neither one was easily able to stay on his feet. A disoriented Paul looked up and tried to get up and join the fray but got kicked by Jessup just under the chin. He collapsed again as round and round the two locked aggressors circled. They appeared to be two marionettes with strings hopelessly entangled.

First bounding off this bulkhead then off that bulkhead, sometimes throwing a punch, sometimes falling to the floor the donnybrook continued until thundering footsteps were heard in the wide-open companionway outside the room. Paul regained himself and struggled to get halfway to his feet before a cabinet crashed over him. It sent the unfortunate boatsman again to the floor.

*Attack of the Koto Maru*

Admiral Ingram looked in the open doorway at the moment Jessup knocked Mark off to the side sending him spinning. The graceless rear admiral quickly rushed over to casing number six, glanced back at the crowd and put a pointy finger on the red button. With Admiral Ingram, Mark, Susan, Naoki and a large security contingent looking on, Jessup began his final hurrah.

"Glad you made it, Admiral. This is it you bastards, welcome to hell!"

Horrified, everyone grimaced and wondered if they'd done well enough on earth to be welcomed into heaven. Each in his own way made their peace and wondered about the unsuspecting Japanese about to be blown up again. Chagrin hit everyone at once. Jessup pushed the red button.

Except for a click, nothing happened. He pushed it again...nothing. The fright in the air was palpable but nowhere was anguish more sorely felt than in the purple furious face of ex-Rear Admiral Jessup hammering away on the button. His anger peaking, he lunged for his gun. Mark was there first. Everyone looked at one another. The drama was over. Jessup had hooked it up wrong.

\* \* \*

In the days after the near catastrophe aboard a nameless freighter, in a crowded harbor, in a busy city, the socio-political world got a good jolt of comeuppance regarding weapons of mass destruction. The incident in Tokyo Bay brought a further consciousness to all governments which in the past had built or harbored nuclear bombs, and it caused each to rethink the importance of even bothering with them. Conferences were scheduled to be held almost everywhere to lay down the rules of eventual disarmament for the world...at least disarmament from A-bombs. Admiral Ingram was delighted to have been a part of the whole thing, and the very incident itself brought much attention to his own conference in Tokyo, now a part of history and a smashing success.

*Alan De Wolfe*

Naoki went on another shopping spree equalled in volume only by perhaps twenty or more buyers from Macy's of New York. He finally exhausted the novelty of it and decided it would be his last outing for awhile. It was soon locked away in giant suitcases. Susan shopped for wedding clothes and tried to avoid invitations to speak at Japan's new women's lib groups. Captain Matsumoto and the crew of the <u>Koto Maru</u> were given a last going away party on a huge motor yacht and told to take the boat home with them as a gift to the island - something to put in their empty quay - along with a second one for good measure. Paul's little skiff was being completely reconditioned right there in the harbor and plans were made for him, Ningo and two other islanders to sail it back to the home archipelago. The households of Timano kept vigil around their repaired short-wave radio for news, anxious to welcome their men back to an island which would never be quite the same again.

Mark decided to help Paul with his book about the adventure which intentionally required him to be in the islands a lot. The lieutenant also learned from his uncle he was to be prematurely retired because the state department decided he'd done enough for his country. All in all everything turned out alright, except for Jessup who'd never see daylight again and the dastardly Ranar, whose case comes to rapid trial two months from now at the World Court in Brussels.

Prior to their departure for different destinations, the group gathered for one last meeting at the Oriental Prince restaurant just down the street from the Imperial Theater. Crowds had stopped pestering them but they still dined free nearly every place they went and everybody knew them. The fairy tale was finished except for their good friendships ahead.

"The biggest relief to me was the fact that Jessup didn't hook up the wiring correctly," Mark offered.

Paul piped in, "I'll say! His last stand even muted the effect of the tsunami - may I never see either one again!"

Naoki grinned and said, "I have the most wonderful thing that has ever happened to me - Susan." Rethinking he added,

"And you guys, of course." Susan smiled and nudged his cheek with hers. She held her glass up as if to toast and said:

> "Here's to us unusual gems. We don't ride in buses,
> we ride on top of thems!"

Her wisdom was followed by a group-groan heard perhaps as far away as Timano.

Printed in the United States
4993